SARAH

HINT
of her BLOOD

CLAWS AND FANGS BOOK 4

Copyright © 2022 by Sarah Spade

All rights reserved.

No part of this book may be reproduced in any form or by any electronic or mechanical means, including information storage and retrieval systems, without written permission from the author, except for the use of brief quotations in a book review.

Cover by Zeki of Phoenix Design Studio

FOREWORD

Thank you for checking out *Hint of Her Blood*!

It might be the fourth book in the **Claws and Fangs** series, but it can also stand as an entry point to this universe since it features a new couple than the previous books. Aleks was an important part of Gem's story, but Elizabeth only made her first appearance in book three, *Forever Mates*.

Now it's her turn to take over as narrator, but if you haven't read the first three books, you can start here and go back to see what happened between Gem and Ryker. Gem's story begins with *Never His Mate*, or you can buy/borrow *Never Say Never*, a collection that features all three books with Gem as the narrator.

As a side note, there are a few passages in this book where the characters are speaking in another language. For example, Aleks speaks Polish, Dominic

FOREWORD

some French, and Roman is Russian. Because this story is told in Elizabeth's POV, there aren't many translations given in the text, though—like previous times Aleks speaks Polish—you can get more insight into this character if you look up what it means :)

In this book, though, I made a conscious stylistic choice not to use the Russian alphabet for when Roman speaks in his native language during his dialogue. This way, the reader can get a better idea of what Elizabeth heard. Just in case you wonder later on in the book, I wanted to put a small note right up front.

Enjoy, and I'm so excited to introduce you to the inner workings of Elizabeth and her Luna-touched wolf!

xoxo,
Sarah

CHAPTER 1

The Western Pack is no more.

Its Alpha is gone, the blond bastard running to plot and plan and fight another day. The Wolf District is quickly becoming an abandoned territory as all of my former packmates follow his lead; some chasing at his heels, others running as far and as fast in the opposite direction as they can. Before long, it won't be safe for a lone wolf to linger on this suddenly unclaimed land, but that realization doesn't do anything to change my mind.

I'm not leaving until I find my treasured cards.

Two years ago, Jack Walker decided that I wouldn't need them. Why would I? In the district, the Alpha provided for all of his packmates. We had food and shelter, plus a barter system for goods. The cards might've been my only way to earn human money while I was a lone wolf, but no one in the district used currency. And if his insistence that I turn over the only possession I held dear to him was a red flag wagging in front of me and my wolf, I ignored it because I had been so desperate just to belong to another pack.

Even if the last two times had ended in disaster, I held out hope that the third time would be the charm.

Oh, Luna, was I wrong about *that*.

The Wicked Wolf took my cards because he could. Because he expected obedience, that no one would ever deny him anything. He took my cards because he wanted to make it harder for me to leave, and even when I accepted that I never could, he kept them if only to remind me just how much power he held over me.

He was the Alpha, and I... I was *other*. I didn't fit anywhere in the pack's hierarchy, and he never let me forget it. I lived only due to his insistence that I would one day take him as my mate. Even when I found the nerve to refuse him, he declared that my special skills belonged to him alone. If he couldn't have me as a chosen mate, then he'd have me as his pet.

For two years, I was just that—until a couple of days ago. Until the Wicked Wolf lost his first ever Alpha challenge and, as a result, lost control of his pack.

I'm free. After so long spent locked in his gilded cage, I can start all over again without the threat of his rough hands, his demands, and his lecherous leer hanging over my head. Maybe, this time, I'll find a pack where they won't discover what I can never quite conceal from other shifters. Or maybe I'll go back to living as a lone wolf, hiding my supe status as I try to exist alongside humans.

I've done it before. I can do it again.

I just need my cards first.

The district is eerily empty. It's only been a little more than forty-eight hours since the Alpha abandoned his territory and already it seems as if the entire pack has disappeared. My ears strain, searching for a hint of another soul as I jog along the wooded border of the main square. Nothing. I'm not that surprised. Gemma and her mate—Henry Wolfson's only pup— left at sun-up this morning. Without the two alphas' presence, the lesser dominant shifters wouldn't stick around.

I should be gone, too. It's not safe here for me—and not just because of my rank in the pack. Gem and Ryker left, taking another pair of Mountainside packmates with them, but that was all.

Which meant that *he* might be long gone, or he could still be somewhere near.

Giving my head a clearing shake, I pour on the

speed. As my jog becomes a sprint, I know it's not just my memories of Walker I'm trying to outrun. If the last two years of being his pet weren't bad enough, this last week alone has been awful and all because of *him*.

Just get the cards, Elizabeth, I tell myself. If they're still in the district, if the Alpha hasn't already gotten rid of them, there's only one place that they'll be. And though I swore to myself that I'd never willingly enter his cabin again, I have to. In the human world, I'll need money. Simple as that. I'll need food and a roof over my head and to get as far away from California as I can. A lone wolf rarely settles down, and though there are other ways I can make a few bucks, I learned a long time ago that my best bet is tarot.

Thanks to my eerie silver gaze and my Luna-given instincts, I don't have to be a true cartomancer. A diviner. *Fortune-teller*. With my weathered tarot cards in hand and a haunted expression, human customers have never doubted my readings. As long as I haven't lost my touch these last couple of years, I'll be able to survive on my own until I figure out what comes next.

Claws crossed.

Now, I don't know what I'm expecting when I make it to the Alpha's cabin. After packing up everything I plan on taking with me when I go, I waited until sundown to make the play for my cards. You'd have to be an idiot—or really, really desperate—to run around an unclaimed shifter territory after dark. Not only is it a magnet to ferals and other scavengers, but it's almost like putting out a welcome mat for the most dangerous kind of supes.

Vampires.

Despite what pop culture says, our ancient enemy isn't weakened by daylight. With the right amount of sunblock, vampires can walk in the sun. But at night... at night is when they're at their strongest.

And it's already well-past sunset.

Make it quick. In and out.

I can do this.

As I slow my run to a quickened walk, I take a deep breath, sampling the scents on the slight breeze. The moon is only beginning to wane again after being full a few nights ago, and she sheds enough light that my shifter's eyes can see everything. For the moment, at least, I'm alone.

Thank the Luna.

With a bit of a hitch in my breath, I head right for the back door to the Alpha's cabin; even knowing that the Wicked Wolf is gone can't keep me from avoiding the front. The knob turns easily under my hand. Of course. No one in the district ever locked their doors, and with his power and his reputation, the Alpha wouldn't think twice about leaving an entrance to his cabin open. Why, when anyone and everyone who dared come inside without an invitation would end up another victim in the pit, fighting for their lives?

I don't bother with turning on the light. It would just be a beacon to my presence if anyone else is still around. Besides, there are windows enough that my goddess is guiding me almost as much as my wolf.

I'm doing as well as can be expected. It's not as easy as I hoped, walking around this cabin again... my skin was already crawling even before I entered in through the back door. My poor wolf was whining at me to stay away the whole time I was running, to heed the layers and layers of warnings in the territorial markings that surrounded the towering structure, retreating deep inside of me as I pushed past them.

She doesn't understand why I'm so attached to a particular set of tarot cards. And I know that I could "read" palms as easily as my cards, but that's not the point. I've carried that deck with me for more than a decade, ever since I left my home pack when I was barely eighteen, and I'll regret it if I don't at least *try* to find them.

Gulping back my discomfort, I close my eyes. Two years is a long time for a scent to cling to a worn deck of cards, but I'm not just searching for a hint of my scent. I don't own much—I haven't since I left my home pack—but anything that I've imprinted on doesn't just carry my scent on it. Courtesy of my "gift", it bears the mark of the Luna.

My eyes spring open. It's faint, but it's there. Somewhere above my head, I can sense her power.

Without even a second thought, I go after it. Though my hackles are up, my wolf reminding me that I shouldn't be here in the Alpha's cabin, I ignore my growing unease as I go. It's so different from the single-floor, two-room cabin I've called mine up until recently, and I can't help but peer around me as I look for the stairs.

The only time I've ever been inside his cabin before now was about a week after I stumbled onto the hidden territory. I'd known him as Jack Walker, Alpha of the Western Pack, then; it wasn't until much later that I realized he was the infamous Wicked Wolf of the West. Forever on the run, I'd needed community. Safety. Security. He'd offered all that and more when he said I could stay in the Wolf District instead of being kicked back out—or worse, I discovered later. Still naively trusting that an Alpha who ruled over hundreds of devoted packmates meant that he was *good*, I jumped at the chance.

Silly, Elizabeth. I should've known better by then that anything that seemed too good to be true often was.

When I agreed to join the pack, he told me to come to his cabin. That he had details he wanted to discuss with me.

He invited me into a spartan kitchen. I thought it

was because the Alpha had no need to cook. Nope. Unfortunately, I was wrong about that, too; when it came to Jack Walker, I was wrong about a lot. In a reversal of how true packs work, he demanded that his packmates tend to *him*, cooking every meal for the Alpha while he lorded over his table in the district square.

Food has always had a special meaning to us shifters. So what if he hadn't prepared it himself? He told me to sit at his table, giving me food to eat. I knew then that I was in big, big trouble. That night was the first time he proposed a partnership. I didn't have a mate. His fated mate was bonded to another male. Why shouldn't we choose each other?

I stammered and stumbled and thought of any excuse to keep from accepting the meal—and his unexpected proposal. I hadn't known then that he was well aware that my unusual eyes meant I was Luna-touched; I'd only seen it as the most powerful wolf in the pack wanted to bond with me. It was much easier to refuse his offer once he admitted he knew the truth, but though he eventually conceded that I wouldn't be his mate, being his pet... it wasn't any better.

At least I didn't have to join him in his cabin. Like with any pack, the Alpha's cabin was reserved for his mate. Jack Walker made lovers of nearly every female in the pack, but always in their home. In fact, I think I might be one of only a few who ever set paw inside of the cabin at all.

It's not just the kitchen that is empty. His whole cabin is like that. Probably because he thought of every home in the district as an extension of his, staying with his lover of the hour before finding another to satisfy his substantial appetites.

We're shifters. We fight and we fuck, and the Wicked Wolf did more of both than any male I've ever met. Even if I wanted a mate, I never could've tamed him. He would've been the death of me.

Honestly, he still might be.

Our laws are clear: an Alpha that loses a challenge is no Alpha. Without a pack to lead, Walker's vicious wolf will be looking for a way to regain control, to continue his cause. How much do you want to bet he'll be looking for a Luna-touched female to conceal his scent to do so? To threaten his enemies with the one thing we all hold dear?

He'll be coming for me. I failed him when he needed me the most, and if I've learned anything about Walker these last two years, he's going to make me pay for it.

Gritting my teeth, trying to ignore just how creepy his empty cabin is, I follow the trace of the Luna up the stairs and down the hall. I'm not surprised when I ease open the door and see the giant bed taking up much of the space. It reeks of the Alpha's musk, but no one else. Just like I thought, he kept all of the females he took out of his cabin.

That makes this a little easier. Against his dark scent, the brightness of the Luna is like a true beacon.

Next to the bed, there's a tall obsidian nightstand that gleams despite the shadows in his room. If they're anywhere, my cards are in there.

On the wall, hanging over the nightstand, I see a massive framed picture. I can't tell if it's a painting or a blown-up photo—or what it's of, actually, since the picture has been slashed to the point it's nearly in tatters. Though my wolf is spurring me to get this over with, I can't stop myself from grabbing the largest piece of torn canvas.

It's a painting, I discover. Of a pretty brunette with golden eyes and a kind smile. And though I've never met her before, I know exactly who this must be: Janelle Booker, the Wicked Wolf's fated mate who rejected him in favor of another Alpha before she was forever bonded to him.

That was twenty-five years ago. Now, Walker is no romantic. He's ruthless and cruel, and if he has a painting of his former mate on the wall of his bedroom, it's only because he gets a kick out of slashing it with his claws.

That's the kind of male I have to avoid. I dodged

the bullet of being forced into a mating with him, but I'd be a fool if I thought he'd let me go.

With my abilities, he never will. And if my instincts are right, he's not the only one...

Another shake. Rougher than the one before if only because I'm running out of time. I've been in here too long, and I don't even have my cards yet.

The nightstand has two drawers. I tug on the first one, gagging when my shifter's sight picks up on the distinct white pieces inside of it.

It's a drawerful of teeth.

No. Not teeth.

Fangs. *Vampire* fangs.

As I stare down at them in surprise mingled with horror, I can't help but think back to the strange conversation I had with the former Alpha's daughter yesterday. Before Gem left the district, she tried to convince me to follow her and her Alpha mate back East.

Yeah, *no*. I tried that once before. It hadn't worked.

She didn't push when I refused. As if sensing how skittish my wolf is these days, she gave me her phone number after explaining that she had a couple of options for me. I could join the Mountainside Pack in Accalia, or even stay at her personally owned townhouse in the nearby city of Muncie.

For some reason, she seemed very interested in

getting me to agree to visit her in the Fang City. And not just her, either.

Him.

Still reeling over how I broke my promise to her, my first instinct had been to thank her, but immediately pass on her offer. She was still determined, though, and as I made my escape, she had called after me, mentioning *his* name.

Aleksander. The fierce yet beautiful vampire that I still can't get out of my head.

She'd said, "If Aleks offers you his fang—"

"His *what*?" It had come out as a squeal. I couldn't help it.

She grinned. "You'll see. *When* he does, do me a favor? Make him explain, but then take it." With a glimmer in her golden eyes, Gem had promised, "You won't regret it."

I'd had no idea what to say to that, so I didn't say anything. I couldn't understand why she thought Aleks —Walker's captive, and Gem's good friend from back East—would give me a fang of all things, but now that I'm looking at a drawer full of them…

I grab a handful, shoving them into the front pocket of my jeans. After closing the drawer, I yank on the second. A sigh of relief escapes when I see the familiar design of the wooden box I've always kept my cards in. Then, because I don't trust the Wicked Wolf at all, I slide it open, double-checking that it isn't empty.

Thank the Luna, it's not. Quickly, I jam the box in my back pocket. It's a tight fit, but I manage.

That done, I slam the second drawer closed before dashing from the room. I've gotten what I came here for—plus more—and now it's time to get my packed bag and get out of the district before it's too late.

With my cards in my pocket, I'm more reckless than I should be. I'm careful while tiptoeing back downstairs, just in case anyone followed me into the Alpha's cabin, but once I'm outside again, I exhale softly.

"Elizabeth?"

I choke on my next inhale.

My mistake. I didn't pay attention to my surroundings as I slipped out of the back again, or even use my nose to see if anyone was lurking nearby.

A dark-haired male moves out of the trees, loping toward the cabin before I can shift or bolt.

It's Brendan. A delta wolf, and one of Walker's soldiers. What is he doing here?

"Elizabeth... I didn't know you were still in the district. I thought everyone was gone."

"So did I," I murmur, trying to calm my suddenly racing heart. To another shifter, it must sound like a beating drum.

It'll also sound like *weakness.*

He doesn't say anything about me stepping out of the cabin, even though it's obvious that that's where I just came from.

Instead, he gives me a boyish grin that doesn't do much to help my nerves as he stared down at me in a way that has my wolf on her guard.

"I'm glad you haven't yet—and I'm glad I saw you tonight when I was getting ready to head out. I mean, I know it's not fate, not really, but it sure seems like it. Don't you think?"

What does that mean, I wonder before answering him with a non-committal, "Oh?"

"Well, yeah. The Luna as my witness, I've been working toward approaching you for a while. It just never seemed like the right time because of your pack status. Now, if I don't, I'll never get another chance and that just doesn't sit right with my wolf."

Uh-oh. I think I know where this is going.

Great.

To make it worse, Brendan says his showing up at the cabin isn't fate. To my suspicious wolf, that just means that he arranged this meeting. Did he stalk me across the district? Why in the Luna's name would he do that? I think I've said maybe three words to Brendan in the two years I've been in the Wolf District, but the look he's giving me...

I keep my expression friendly even as I fight the urge to turn tail and run. "Talk to me? About what?"

His golden eyes darken just a touch. Lust is a sudden slick coating the night air. Even before he begins to explain, I know my earlier suspicions were correct.

That doesn't stop Brendan. Taking a few steps closer to me, careful as if he can tell that my wolf is different, is *other*, and can be either skittish or brutal... he approaches like I'm a wounded wolf caught in a trap.

In so many ways, I *am*.

"You were always so protected by the Alpha," he says softly, "and when he didn't claim you as his, I thought maybe... maybe you were free to be claimed by another. Willing, too. I was hoping to tell you that my wolf was interested in yours, but then there was Theo..." Lifting his hand, he runs his fingers through his shaggy, dark brown hair. His claws leave track marks in the thick strands. "Well, after what happened with him, he's out of the running. But maybe... maybe I could be. In it, I mean. 'Cause I know we have to go. If you want, maybe we could head out together."

His voice is gentled. Soothing. The lust, though? It's as dark as the look in his eyes.

Why do I get the idea that, if I say no, he'll follow behind me anyway?

This is just my luck. Is this why he's still hanging around the district even though it seems like everyone else is already gone? Using my wolf's instinct, I guess he seems earnest enough, like he really means it. Like he really wants me to choose him.

And while I have to admit that my wolf assures me that he's no danger to either of us, I never would've guessed he had any interest in me. I have no idea where any of this is coming from, especially after what happened the last couple of days.

A couple years younger than my twenty-nine, Brendan was born and raised to serve his Alpha. Since coming of age at eighteen, he's been a loyal soldier to the Wicked Wolf's cause. He would never make a move on me if he thought I had his Alpha's eye.

And Theo...

I don't know if you'd call it a blessing or a curse, but my "gift" doesn't just allow me to break bonds. It also gives me an insight when one might be possible. Not all mates are fated, and if a chosen pairing has potential, I can feel it like a chilled whisper on the back of my neck.

I've known of Theodore Michaels for almost as long as I've been in the Wolf District. He was the odd alpha who was submissive enough to serve another devotedly, a position that saved his hide as Beta after Beta failed the Alpha of the Western Pack. He survived, rising to the highest ranks within the pack. Whenever Walker was between Betas, he used Theo as his errand boy, so I got to know him pretty well since he was often the one sent to drag me in front of the Alpha whenever he had need of me.

While Brendan's interest is undeniably genuine, Theo barely seemed to notice I was a female. I'd thought it was because I made the Wicked Wolf believe that I *couldn't* have a bond with another male, so why would any wolf in his inner circle pay any attention to me as more than his pet?

In fact, never once did Theo turn his fake smile and calculating eyes on me—until a couple of months ago when the rumors of Ruby Walker still being alive began to wind their way through the Western Pack and, suddenly, I could be of use to him.

Ruby Walker... only that isn't her name anymore, is she?

Gemma Swann. The female alpha who threatened to gut me if I did anything to the bond she had with her beloved mate. The same Gem who forgave me when her father ordered me to do just that, if only because I hadn't been able to.

Gem and Ryker's bond is both fated and unbreakable. The Luna blessed them, and not even my touch could break them apart. Still, I had to try because the Alpha commanded me to, and it was impossible to refuse him.

She threatened to gut me, but the Wicked Wolf? He would've done way worse.

Theo wanted Gem. He never wanted *me;* like the

Alpha, he just wanted what I could do for him. If I used my ability to break her bond with Ryker, then Theo could attempt to claim her for himself. But too eager to make her his, he couldn't wait. He challenged Ryker Wolfson, and he lost.

Then Gem challenged her father. He lost, too, though she showed mercy at the end. Theo is dead while Jack Walker lives on.

I already have him to worry about. Brendan's proposal is a complication that I don't need.

And that's not all...

His scent reaches me before I see him. Brendan's considerable bulk shielded him from my sight, but once I pick up on that icy, chilly aura, I shift to the side, looking past the shifter to spy the vampire in the not-too-far distance.

How long has he been there? Where did he come from?

And, most importantly, what is he doing here?

I should've expected this. When he didn't leave with Gem and her packmates, I told myself it was because he fled as soon as she freed him from the cage that the Alpha had thrown him in. Why would a captive vampire want to stick around any longer than he had to? I had thought he might already be on the trail of the Wicked Wolf, looking for his revenge.

But he isn't. He's here, towering in the distance, watching me so closely, I can't stifle my shiver.

I slip my shaky hand with its trembling fingers into my pocket, searching for the fangs. Squeezing them against my palm, I pray to the Luna that they give me some level of protection against the hungry look in the vampire's blood-red gaze.

There isn't much I know about the bloodthirsty supernaturals, but even I understand that the red eyes are a warning sign. Vampires, as a race, all have light eyes—until their thirst takes over and their irises turn red.

And unless he's had a meal since Gemma ran the Alpha off two days ago, he has to be very, very thirsty.

If I'm being honest, though, fear of his bite isn't what has me staring back at him, unable to look away. Taking in his beautiful form isn't, either, though Luna knows he's gorgeous even after a week of captivity.

The moon shines down, illuminating his sculpted features. His hair is tousled in soft-looking caramel-colored curls, the tips of his fangs peeking over his lush bottom lip. Strangely enough, his hands are clenched into tight fists at his side while his expensive-looking shirt is still riddled with bullet holes.

He's not only gorgeous. He's awe-inspiring.

And he's supposed to be *mine*.

Brendan falls away; he's still standing in front of me, but it's like he doesn't exist at all. At that moment, it's just me and a vampire who looks at me like he knows me—and who I instinctively recognize in return.

Yours, whispers the Luna.

Mine, I agree—

No. *No.*

Never.

I'm a wolf shifter. He's a bloodsucker. I'm damaged goods, and he... well, according to Gem, he has his own baggage, doesn't he?

Like the fact that the Alpha of my pack had him captured, shot repeatedly, caged, then forced to fight for his life.

Is that what he's doing here now? Vampires don't worship the Luna like shifters do. Even if I recognize who he's supposed to be to me, there's no guarantee that he feels the same. For all I know, he's been haunting the district, attacking any of us who stayed behind before targeting our former Alpha.

The murderous look he shoots Brendan makes me suspect I'm not too far off base with that thought.

Swallowing roughly, I tear my gaze away from him. Mumbling some excuse to Brendan, I purposely turn my back on both males. My wolf yips, telling me that I should go to *him*. When I refuse, she goes silent.

It's better this way, I tell her. If he really thought of us as his mate, he would be moving toward us instead of gliding away again.

Which he is.

I reach out with my senses, subtly sniffing the air. An electric pulse courses through my body, fading as his presence does. His lingering scent hangs on the breeze, but it's only a tease.

When I look behind me again, he's gone. Brendan, too, but I barely notice his absence.

Oh, no. Just like my wolf, I'm only concerned with the vampire, but he's gone.

And if I'm lucky, I'll never see him again.

CHAPTER 2

FIVE MONTHS LATER

Does it ever stop snowing in Muncie?

Letting the curtain slip from my fingers, I sigh.

My bedroom overlooks the back of the townhouse. I've learned that, depending on the wind, snow piles up faster out there. Considering there have been more wintry days than not since I moved here, there was a good four or five inches already back there. After today's storm? There are probably another three more.

I'm quickly becoming sick of it—and it's only February 3rd. Yesterday was Groundhog Day. The furry little rodent supposedly didn't see his shadow so that means that we should have an early spring.

I really freaking hope so.

I'm a West Coast female. As a shifter, my fur coat is a part of me. The winter chill doesn't affect me the same way it does the humans, but I'm used to living in California. It was nice to see snow at first, but if I never did again, that would be perfectly fine, too.

It's been snowing since early morning. I keep hoping it will stop since, for the first time in days, I actually have plans to leave the townhouse.

It hasn't.

Ugh.

Out of habit, I cross the bedroom and pick up my tarot deck, absently shuffling the familiar worn cards. Since I arrived in the Fang City two weeks ago, I haven't had to use them. As a welcome gift, Gem stocked the refrigerator and cabinets with food, telling me she was paying me back for the food she ate from my kitchen during her stay in the Wolf District so that I wouldn't feel a certain way about the younger female trying to feed me. As if I would. If I was already accepting shelter from her, I'd only be spiting myself—and my wolf—if I refused the food.

I don't know how many strings she pulled so that I could live among the vampires. Plenty, I'm sure. A Fang City is supposed to be as tight-knit and protective of a community as a shifter pack, only for vampires instead. As a shifter—the vampire race's ancient supe enemy—I decided not to risk provoking them. Just in case, I've been choosing to stay inside of my own personal territory whenever I could.

It's the first time in forever that I've actually had a permanent address. I'm going to enjoy it for as long as it lasts.

For five months, I traveled all across the country, never settling in one place for long in case the Wicked Wolf sniffed me out. I haven't been able to forget how he threatened to go to the Alpha collective about me. If I betrayed him, if I ever tried to leave his pack, he would tell them that I was an abomination. He promised I'd be put down, and even though Gem tried to convince me that they would understand I'm not to blame for my abilities, I've always made other supes uneasy.

I hate to see what vampires would do if they realized what I was, and what I'm capable of. And if I used that as an excuse to reject Gemma's offer of a place to stay over and over again since our time together in the Wolf District, I'd rather cling to that than the real reason I stayed away from the East Coast for so long.

By December, though, I... I just couldn't do it anymore. It was harder to find tourists who wanted a street performer to read tarot cards for them during the holidays, and the overwhelming loneliness that settled over me while I was on the run became unbearable.

My wolf wanted her mate, and I wanted to pretend

I never discovered that Aleksander Filan was fated to be mine.

I celebrated Christmas in a roach-infested motel, the only type I could afford. By January, I was spending more and more time in my fur when the last of my money ran out. Then, one day, I swore I picked up something on a whisper of a breeze. A scent that made my wolf keen and my heart sing. Looking back, I'm sure it was an olfactory hallucination, but I'd lost all will to fight my other half sometime around the middle of January.

I called Gem, and I accepted her offer. Within days, she gave me the okay. I moved into the townhouse that Ryker Wolfson gave her as a mating gift two weeks ago with a single duffel bag stuffed with my belongings, a pocketful of vampire fangs, my tarot deck, and a determination that I wouldn't track down my mate.

I didn't have to.

He found *me*.

Of all supes, vampires have a distinctive scent. It's a mixture between meat and the icy chill of death, but it's not... unpleasant. Maybe it's because, deep down, I'm a predator, it doesn't really bother me. Of course, because of the way shifters are wired, scenting a vampire is enough to put our backs up. You sniff a vampire, you know that there's a threat.

When I scent Aleks, I'm in even more trouble.

That night outside of the Alpha's cabin in the Wolf

District was the last time I've seen him. But, the morning after I moved into the townhouse, I started noticing something on the sidewalk out front. Thanks to the snow, it's impossible to hide every and all tracks, and no matter if it's slushy, crusty, or freshly fallen powder, when I wake up in the morning, there's a pair of footprints positioned perfectly before my door, as if someone has stood guard like a sentinel over me as I slept.

At first, I refused to believe it. But that's the thing when it comes to being a shifter. The footprints make it easy to tell that someone's been there, but I don't need them. His scent lingers, so I know exactly who watches me.

It's the same scent that I still want to believe I imagined in a dry forest in Arizona.

Aleks.

He knows I'm a shifter. My nose might not be as strong as some others, but I'd have to be completely stuffed up to miss the way his scent hovers inside of my own territorial markers.

He's a vampire. From what I understand, his own keen senses would have noticed that my markers are so very different than Gem's were. Even if he doesn't know it's *me* living here, it's sure as hell not Gem.

So the footprints? I decided a week ago that they were deliberate. They have to be. Though he's never made it a point to meet me face to face, he's stopped by my townhouse every night since I arrived, and he wants me to *know* that.

Too bad I have no idea what to make of his intentions. If he was a wolf, I'd understand, but he's a vampire. For all I know, it could be a threat.

I tried to be suave. Casual. Anytime I spoke to Gem, I made it seem like an afterthought before I inevitably mentioned Aleks. It was almost as if I was incapable of forgetting about him, and considering their history, she was the only one I could talk to about him.

I learned that he wasn't just an unlucky vampire who got caught along the edge of the district. He was her former roommate, one of her closest friends, and he was in California because Ryker asked him to keep Gem safe while she was matching wits with the Wicked Wolf. When cornered, he could be a vicious killer, but he spoke six languages fluently, wore a pair of glasses when he read his favored thrillers in paperback form, and was one of the most respected vampires in all of Muncie.

And, five months after I first laid eyes on him, the Luna is still whispering insistently that he's my mate—though he's made no move to let me know that he feels any kind of pull toward me in return.

The only way I could deal with knowing he was watching me was by convincing myself that it was a security thing. A member of the Cadre, of course he'd want to make sure that the unfamiliar shifter in their territory wasn't a threat to anyone else.

Especially since he knows I came from the Western Pack. It might be disbanded now, but its reputation is still alive and kicking. For all I know, Aleks thinks I'm just as sadistic as the Wicked Wolf.

Of course he's keeping a careful eye on me.

Right?

This afternoon is no different. Though the snow covers his tracks from last night, I can still make out the vague dips where the new snow piled up on the old snow before filling in the center of his footprint.

His scent is faded, but undeniable. Feeling silly but unable to stop myself, I breathe in deep as I pass his stationed spot after I head out into the lingering flurries. The only way to get to the downtown area where I can find Charlie's is by walking right by it. Besides, I don't want him to think that he's the reason why I rarely leave the townhouse.

At least, not the *only* reason...

I'd known for a while that this was something I would have to do. I might not be able to use my tarot cards to make money, but Gem did me another favor by contacting the vampire owner of the supe bar where she worked for a year before moving permanently to Accalia, the mountain settlement where her pack lives. Charlie was always looking for new help, and he got along great with Gem. All I needed to do was go down to the bar tonight when he was actually there, talk to him about the job, and hopefully I won't have to worry about how I'm going to support myself in Muncie any longer.

I've been worried for days now. My meager savings is long gone, and though I don't need much, I'm pretty sure stealing is frowned upon in the Fang City.

I need a job.

As I scurry, careful not to slip on the slick snow since I didn't have any boots to put on, I bow my head against the wind; the cold doesn't bother me, but the snow stinging my eyes is freaking annoying. On the plus side, I do have a coat and a scarf on to help me hide out among the humans. My hood is pulled over my hair, tugged as low as possible to cover the way my silver eyes seem to reflect the snowflakes.

Last thing I need is a human to notice and start staring. They're everywhere in the Fang City. Obviously. I mean, vampires have got to eat, don't they?

I don't bother hiding from them, though. No matter what, they—like all other supes—can sense there is something different about me. Not just that I'm a shifter, either, but *other*.

Case in point? A towering vampire who is walking out of Charlie's just as I'm approaching the bar.

It has the owner's name stenciled on the window, so I know I've found the right place, but I was too busy looking at it to notice that the glass door was being pulled open, a vampire stalking out into the snow.

We don't quite touch, though that has more to do with his reflexes than mine.

Even beneath the white sky, I see his eyes flash, going from an almost icy blue to a deep red. Ducking my head even further, shielding my odd silver gaze, I tamp down my own innate scent. While I wouldn't say being Luna-touched has a ton of perks—the Luna pops into my head like an unwelcome conscience at the weirdest of times, and having the power to snap mate bonds makes me an outcast among my kind—being able to conceal my scent is one of them.

He does a double-take, shaking his head, then continues walking down the street.

I slip inside, grateful that I made it to the bar without any real incident.

Shaking the snow off, I pull my hood down, glancing around. Gem told me that Charlie rarely spent time out on the floor, so I should look for a human bartender named Hailey instead. She would smell like a mixture of blood, vampire, and vanilla, but if the overwhelming scents surrounding the bar were too much, I should look for a vampire bite on a pretty brunette.

Her description is spot-on. Almost immediately, the dark-haired human female behind the bar—wearing a half-healed vampire bite on her throat like a badge of honor—looks up, almost as if she was expecting me.

She comes rushing out from behind the bar. "Hi there. I'm Hailey. You must be Elizabeth."

As she grabs my hand, I stiffen. I'm not used to other people touching me. My packmates would never dare, and the customers I often did tarot readings for always kept their distance.

But she's friendly enough, and I don't want to give off a bad first impression if she's going to be my co-worker so I don't say anything as she tells me that Charlie is already waiting for me in their storeroom behind the bar.

Hailey leads me there, pointing out the door I need to take, then returns to talking to one of the customers at the bar.

Praying to the Luna that this goes well, I let myself in.

Most vampires appear ageless, but Charlie is one of those odd ones who turned late in life and must've stubbornly kept their grump. There's no other way to explain it. He's got a thick middle, a deep scowl, and eyes that are a muted brown. I don't get the feeling that the scowl is for me, though. Charlie is just one of those people who looks pissed off at the world no matter what.

I offer him a wave. "Hi. I'm Elizabeth."

"Come on in."

I try not to be too nervous as I walk into the cramped room. A massive fridge stands across from me, a desk in one corner, and shelves full of all kinds of supplies take up two of the four walls.

Gem assured me that this is just a formality. She vouched for me with her old boss and her co-workers, and so long as I didn't screw this up too badly, the job is mine.

There are two folding chairs set up in the middle of the space5. Charlie is sitting in one, then he points to the other.

I sit down.

"So, Gem tells me that you're a friend of hers."

Huh. I guess I am. "Yes."

"And you need a job."

"Yes," I say again. That one is way more emphatic.

"Okay. Let's talk about what I expect from my employees. I'll ask you a couple of questions to make sure you're a good fit. Then we'll go from there. What do you think?"

I swallow back my nerves. "Sounds good."

"Great."

For the next ten minutes, Charlie does just that. It's very informal, and I see exactly what Gem meant when she said that I didn't have to be nervous. He might be the owner, but he's not the type to micromanage. He wants a team that knows what they're doing and doesn't cause any problems for him.

In the middle of his explaining exactly what hours he's looking to fill behind the bar, his nostrils flare a split second before there's a rap at the door.

He doesn't even have to ask who it is. He just calls out, "Come in, Tony."

A human male pokes his head in. "Hey, boss. You busy?"

The vampire's gaze flickers over to me. "I'm in the middle of an interview. Got someone to take over Gem's spot. Why? What is it?"

"One of the Cadre wants to speak with you."

"Who?"

"Zakharov's right-hand man."

Charlie doesn't even hesitate. "Tell him I'll be right out."

Now, I'm not too well-versed in vampire politics. All I know is that the Cadre controls Muncie. They're in charge of keeping the peace—and, for the most part, the secret of supernaturals—and they protect everyone who lives in the Fang City. Made up of the most powerful vampires in Muncie, they uphold the laws and protect the citizens from any outside threats.

The main way they do this is through patrols. Most vampires and humans have a free pass to come and go from the city, but non-vampire supes like me aren't allowed at all. For twenty-four hours a day, the Cadre employs dedicated vampires who do constant perimeter checks, making sure that no threats breach the borders.

The vampires all respect those who are part of the Cadre. If one of their number is here to talk to Charlie, that definitely trumps my interview with him.

After telling me to sit tight, that he'll be right back, he heads back out into the bar.

I sit anxiously on the edge of my seat as I wait for him to return, grateful that this is just a formality.

CHAPTER 3

Some formality.

Charlie finishes the "interview" about five minutes after he finally comes back into the backroom. I don't even know why he bothers. There are no more questions, just half-hearted excuses why he doesn't think I'm a good fit for the bar. Cheeks flaming from the rejection, I just nod along, barely listening as he stands up from his chair.

Automatically, I rise. He tells me that he'll keep me in mind, and if another position opens up, I'll be the first to call. Since I know he's only saying that because he can sense my raging disappointment, I pull a gracious smile to my face, then thank him for his time.

As I walk out of the backroom, my head is already spinning as I try to figure out what I'm going to do next.

I can't perform tarot readings in the city. My whole act relies on unwitting humans who have no idea that supes really exist. Half of my customers are sure I'm a fraud, while the other half believe I have a real gift; either way, they're entertained and I'm paid. The ones who think I'm a fraud... they're pretty spot-on. I'm not a fortune-teller. I'm a shifter who uses her wolf to pick up on little things about the customer I'm reading. A racing heart, a nervous chuckle, how a scent changes... if I can't read the cards for real, at least I can read body language. After all these years, I can spin any card to give the customer the experience they're after.

No one would buy that here. At best, they'd figure out I was some kind of supe. In our world, there are plenty of different types of supes, though the main ones are shifters and vampires. Claws and fangs. My silver eyes and concealed scent might cover me for a bit, but it's obvious I'm not a bloodsucker; if I'm not a vampire, with my power level, it doesn't take a genius to figure out that I must be a shifter. And the number one rule I agreed to when I moved into Muncie was hiding what I was so I don't inadvertently start another war between our peoples.

They happen. Claws and Fangs wars... over the thousands of years that we have considered each other enemies, brutal skirmishes were inevitable. The last great war happened over two hundred years ago, but with my luck? I'll draw the attention of the wrong vampire and start another one.

No, thanks.

As I slink out from behind the bar, I'm reminded once again that I really shouldn't be here. It had seemed like such a good idea at the time, finally having a place that I could settle down for a while as I decided whether or not to join Gem in the Mountainside Pack. I thought I could deal with being near enough to my mate without acknowledging him. So far, so good on that front.

It's the other vampires that are giving me a problem.

There aren't that many Fang Cities in the States. Because vampires have such a long history with Europe, most of their kind settled there centuries ago and never left. Some of those that did became the equivalent of a lone wolf. As rogues, they hunted on their own, but rarely made it long before the bloodlust took over and the most powerful of vampires had to clean up after them.

But for the vampires who wanted community, who wanted a place where blood was just another transaction, the Fang Cities were born. Each territory is ruled by members of the Cadre, with a single leader that's like their Alpha. Because they're basically food for the vampires, humans are welcome; supes are an open secret in a city like Muncie, but the humans in the know all keep the truth of their vampire rulers from outsiders. The Cadre protects every soul inside their borders, and they're very choosy about who they let inside.

As far as I know, I'm the only non-vampire supe in all of Muncie; definitely the only shifter. I took Gem's place when she passed her townhouse over to me, but that doesn't mean that the vampires who realize my wolfish secret are happy I'm here.

Working with humans—whether they know about supes or not—would only be a disaster. After talking at length with Gem about the city, I got the idea that very few vampires would be willing to hire me. She only got the job behind the bar because Aleksander vouched for her, getting Charlie to agree to give her a chance.

She did the same for me, but it obviously didn't work.

And despite the fact that the Luna insists that Aleks is meant to be mine, it's not like I can ask him for help. With me pretending he doesn't exist, and him stopping by my home but never formally letting me know he's aware of my presence…

I don't even know for sure if he remembers me. He could just be curious about the female who moved into Gem's townhouse. Just because I recognize him as mine doesn't mean he feels the same.

Especially since he spent the last year in love with Gemma...

I huff out a breath. As if I couldn't feel any worse about losing out on the job at Charlie's, that intrusive thought just has to pop into my head.

Again.

Whenever I think about how my mate might be in love with another shifter, my stomach goes tight, my throat raw. It took weeks into our friendship before I admitted to Gem that I felt a pull toward Aleks, and she's spent the months after that assuring me that she never reciprocated his feelings. That he told her following what happened in California that he was over her. It still bothers me, even if I wish it wouldn't.

For now, I can't worry about Aleks. If I can't find work, I'll be out of Muncie before this awkward dance we're doing around one another ends with us eventually coming face to face with each other.

Will I still be able to reject him then?

Adjusting my scarf as I prepare to head back out into the snow, I push Aleks out of my head.

Okay. I struck out at Charlie's. Fine. It happens. I should call Gem now. Maybe she has an idea what I can do for a backup.

With that thought in mind, I make a bee-line for the front door. As I do, the male customer—vampire, my wolf warns me—that was chatting with Hailey near the far side of the bar suddenly breaks away from her, heading straight for me.

I'm only aware of him because my wolf subconsciously watches out for vampires whenever I'm walking around in Muncie.

Slipping my hands in my pocket, my fingers stroke the fangs I have in there. They're still the ones I stole from the Alpha's nightstand, and I treat them like a good luck talisman when I'm forced to be around vampires.

Remembering her warning about Aleks offering me one of his, I asked Gem once why Walker would've had a drawer full of them. She couldn't tell me, though she did mention that, in some Fang Cities, carrying one gave you a measure of protection.

Since then, I've had at least three in my pocket at all times.

Just as I'm pushing against the glass door, eager to get the hell out of the bar, he calls out my name.

I freeze.

Please, oh please, let there be another Elizabeth in here…

Before I know it, he's right behind me. "Excusez moi. You are Elizabeth Howell, yes?"

My heart sinks.

I glance over my shoulder at him. Like all vampires, his skin is flawless, his features inhumanly divine. His blond hair is styled precisely in one of those two hundred dollar haircuts. His suit probably cost more than all my wardrobe combined.

"Uh. Yeah. That's me."

"Bon. My name is Dominic Le Croix. I've been sent to retrieve you."

What? "I... I don't know what you mean."

"I work for the Cadre. Roman wants to see you. I'm to bring you to him right now."

Did I think today couldn't get any worse? "Roman?" I repeat. "You don't mean Roman—"

"Zakharov, yes."

I might be a shifter, but even I know who *that* is.

And I'm utterly screwed if he's sent one of his patrollers after me.

Now, Gem has wanted me to join her pack since we met when she came to confront the Wicked Wolf, her birth father. Mountainside is aptly named. The shifters turned the sides and the top of a mountain into a protected community called Accalia. But I... I just wasn't ready to join a pack again. I was a lone wolf for eight years. The only two times that I allowed myself to believe I could go back to pack living were disasters. Kyle fooled me, and Walker captured me.

After two years in the Wolf District, I looked forward to being free again. But without any family, any money, any roots... it sucked. Sucked even more once I learned who my fated mate was meant to be.

I guess it was inevitable that I'd end up in Muncie. I gave it a good shot, but I couldn't stay away.

When I accepted her offer to stay in the townhouse, she gave me a crash course in living inside of a Fang City. Apart from making sure I understood that most—though not all—vampires hate shifters instinctively, the biggest thing she impressed upon me was never to get on the wrong side of Roman Zakharov.

He's basically the vampire's Alpha. What he says goes, and I'm only allowed to live within Muncie's borders because he agreed.

And now he wants to see me?

That can't be good.

I'VE NEVER BEEN TO THE CENTER OF MUNCIE BEFORE AND for good reason, too. The Cadre—the vampire-run government in charge of the bloodsuckers, their donors, and the humans who have no idea what goes bump in the night around them—controls every element of the bordered settlement, but it is headquartered in the exact middle of the city.

Their towering headquarters is named, aptly enough, the Cadre building. Very simple. Very self-explanatory. From the outside, there's no way to tell that it's effectively the most important structure in the Fang City with one exception: every single window on the twenty-five-story building is blacked out.

Perfect for vampires.

Dominic offered to drive me over, but I suggested we walk. The two miles between Charlie's and the Cadre building is nothing to a shifter and, like most of my kind, I get a little anxious inside of enclosed spaces. To my wolf, they're too close to being cages.

Cars are out. Trains, too. Buses.

Luckily, Muncie is an urban city similar to Manhattan. It has a great public transport system, but for us supes, walking is not only normal, it's almost expected. Any Cadre member on patrol does it on foot; with stamina and speed almost as impressive as a shifter's, most vampires don't bother with driving when they could be faster without a car.

Dominic agreed to walk, though I get the idea it wasn't his first choice. It takes until we've made it to the heart of Muncie before I figure out why.

The center is full of vampires, and they all sense something different about me. Among humans, I can do a pretty good job of hiding. Walking up to the building? I *can't*.

Smart, Elizabeth. Really smart.

To outrun their murmurs and their stares, I increase my pace, Dominic easily matching it. I let him overtake me as he leads me into the front lobby of the building.

Soft music is playing. Over the noticeable scent of *vampire* that clings to everything in the room, there's a hint of fresh linen being pumped through the vents. Directly in front of us, there's a huge counter that couples as a rounded desk for the stunning vampire sitting behind it.

Her eyes widen when she spots me, but Dominic nods to her. That must mean something because she doesn't say a word as he guides me down the hall that leads past her desk.

"The elevator's this way," he tells me.

My wolf backs up, shaking her head as she whines. I know how she feels. An elevator is just like a car. If I can avoid it, I don't want to go in there.

"Are there any stairs?"

Dominic gives me a curious look. "Roman's office is on the twenty-first floor."

And?

He nods. "Of course. Let me show you."

Together, we take the stairs. The higher we climb, the more I notice a very powerful, very old aura crackling like electricity against my skin. If I wasn't already nervous as hell to meet Roman, that does it.

I knew he was the leader. Now I know why.

Once we exit out on the twenty-first floor, Dominic gestures at a closed door. "He's expecting you."

"You're not coming in with me?"

I don't know why I asked that. He told me he was sent to retrieve me and he did. But... I really don't want to go in there by myself.

Dominic shakes his head. "Not yet. I have something to take care of first, but I'm sure I'll be seeing you soon. Before I go, though..." He holds out his hand, palm up. "The fangs, please."

When I stare at him blankly, he gives my right pocket an impatient nod. "They're in there. I don't know where you got them from or why you have them, but you don't want to offend Roman. In Muncie, you earn a fang. They're gifts. The ones you have are worthless."

Oh my Luna. He knows about the fangs I stole from Walker.

My blush returns as I hurriedly jam my hand in my pocket. Grabbing the three I have stowed in there, I shove them at Dominic. "I'm sorry. I... I didn't know."

"You're not the first to misunderstand how we do things here. It'll be fine. And you don't have to be afraid of Roman. Just don't lie to him, and don't offend him, and everything is going to be okay."

That's easy for him to say. He's not going in there.

I nod. "Thanks."

Then, before I lose my nerve, I grab the doorknob, give it a turn, and push it open.

The force of Roman's aura nearly knocks me over,

it's that strong. It takes a second for me to recover, and when I do?

I'm nearly bowled over again by his appearance.

I'd heard whispers of his name even before I came to live in Muncie. I don't know what I thought he looked like, but I'm definitely not prepared for the male sitting behind his wide, oak desk.

Like most vampires who were fair-skinned before they were turned, his skin is iridescently pale. His hair might've been blond once, but there are so many silver strands poking through his short mane, it nearly sparkles beneath his special vampire-friendly fluorescent lights. He has it parted precisely on the left, the longer hanks of hair swooped over to the right, covering one of his eyes.

The other? It's so pale, it's nearly colorless. I can see the whites of that single eye, his pitch-black pupil, and then... *nothing*.

And they say my silver eyes are creepy. Next time I hear that, I'll have to remember that it can always be worse.

He could be twenty. He could be thirty. He has that ageless sort of classic face that screams *innocence*, though his powerful aura puts him at a couple of hundred years old at least.

And he's looking at me as if he's seen a ghost.

"Julia." He rises from behind the desk, rubbing his chin as the single eye I can see seems to glitter.

Then, almost under his breath, he adds, "Ne mozhet byt'."

His voice is gruffer than I expect from his striking looks, though maybe I just think that because of his notable accent. If I'm not mistaken, it's Russian, which makes sense. With the name of Zakharov, I figured he was probably one of the Eastern Europe vampires.

I have no idea what he just said except for maybe the first word. Though I get the idea he was talking about me, I glance over my shoulder, looking for the Julia he mentioned.

There's no one there.

When he clears his throat, my head swivels forward again. His flawless features are rearranged into a careful mask. The faint expression of surprise when he saw me is gone. In fact, he looks more like how I imagined the immortal leader of a Cadre would.

Hard.

Strong.

Judging.

My wolf goes down on her belly, prepared to bare her throat in submission to Roman. I don't blame her. His aura is as icy cold as every other vampire I've met, but his is... it's different. Like it's so powerful, a single touch would freeze me so completely, I'd burn.

Alpha, I think again. He has fangs, no pulse, and he drinks blood—but, make no mistake, Roman is as much an Alpha as the Wicked Wolf of the West.

As I can't help but stare at him, he nods at me as if he's found something inside of me that's worth his time. Then, after sitting back down, he presses a button on the old-fashioned office phone perched on the corner of his desk. A red light blinks.

"Yes, Roman?"

"Leigh. Tell Dominic I'm ready for him and Felicity, won't you?"

"Right away."

"Thank you."

He releases the button, folding his hands in front of him. "I'm glad you were available to meet with me, Elizabeth. I've been meaning to do this for some time, but I've finally found the perfect opportunity."

"Um. Okay."

I have so many questions. How did he know that I was going to meet Charlie this afternoon? It's Sunday, just before dark, and though it stopped snowing earlier, it's still a mess outside.

And what does he want me for? If Gem got his permission to give me her old townhouse for the time being, he knew where to find me. Sending Dominic to Charlie's could've been coincidental, but I doubt it. For some reason, he didn't want to have one of his vampires approach me on my territory.

Makes sense. I might not be an alpha, but I guard anything I consider mine as ruthlessly as any other shifter.

But, because I'm *not* an alpha, I don't dare ask Roman any of those questions. I just stand in the middle of the office, unsure if I'm supposed to sit down in one of the empty chairs placed in front of his desk. He doesn't invite me to, and I'm not too keen on getting even closer to the powerful vampire.

Yeah... I'm just going to stay right here while we wait for the vampires he called for to appear.

It's not a long wait. Less than five minutes later, the door swings in. Dominic holds it open for a vampire female. Felicity, I assume, who, like every other vampire I've met, looks like she belongs on a runway. She has wavy brown hair that hits her shoulders, a body I'd kill for, and light violet eyes that have me wondering if they're contacts.

She's a vampire. I doubt it.

She enters the office, bowing her head in respect as she greets Roman. Dominic follows her, and while I can sense the bond tying them together, he keeps his distance.

That's interesting.

"Elizabeth," Roman says, calling my attention back to him. "What can you tell me about these two? About their connection?"

It's a test. Obviously. Somehow, he knows exactly what makes me different than every other shifter I've ever known—and I don't just mean the color of my eyes.

"Um. Sure. These two are bonded together." Then, on a guess, I add, "But they don't want to be anymore."

Felicity's head shoots over to me, the surprise doing nothing to make her any less stunning. "That's right. How did you know that?"

"She's been blessed by the shifter goddess," Roman announces, and it's my turn to look over at the head vampire of Muncie in surprise.

Okay. Now how did he know *that*?

He nods at me. "Yes. I know all about your gift, Elizabeth. I've been hoping to see how it works for myself. When Dominic came to me to ask if I'd considered his bonding to Felicity effectively broken, I remembered what I heard about you. I thought you could try to make their separation more permanent."

"I can. I mean, it doesn't always work." Gem was proof of that. "But as long as one of the two bonded mates wants their bond to break, it should."

"What if both of us do?" asks Felicity.

"It was an arranged betrothal," Dominic explains. "She's not my beloved and I'm not hers. I found mine, but I can't claim her fully while I'm still tied to Felicity. It wouldn't be fair to either of them. And Felicity..."

She shakes her head royally. "I'd like the chance to find my own mate. My beloved or one I choose to bond with myself, I'm not picky. I care for Dominic, but I don't love him. We both deserve to be with one that we *do* love."

In that case, it should be easy to break them apart, and I tell them that.

Roman gestures for me to go ahead.

Taking a deep breath, viscerally aware that I'm surrounded by three vampires, I place one hand on Dominic; after our walk to the Cadre building, I'm more comfortable touching him than Felicity. It only takes me touching one half of a bond and I know whether it's unbreakable.

And theirs isn't. Just like that, it's severed in half.

Felicity sighs in relief. Dominic clutches his heart, a determined expression already twisting his classically handsome face.

"It is done?" Roman asks.

Both of the vampires nod.

"Then you're free to go. Elizabeth, I would ask that you stay. But, first... Dominic? I assume you'll be requesting some time off?"

"Uh— yes, sir. If that's fine with you."

"Of course. Congratulations on your new beloved."

"Thank you, Roman." The male vampire turns on me, pure gratitude written all over his face. "And thank you, too, Elizabeth."

Isn't that a first? A supe *thanking* me for breaking their bond? "You're welcome."

With another reverential bow toward their leader, Felicity and Dominic leave his office, each one of them much happier than they were when they entered.

As soon as the door closes behind them again, Roman turns his stare back on me before saying the last thing I expect from the leader of the Cadre:

"I want to hire you."

CHAPTER 4

I blink. I'd been halfway convinced that he was going to boot me from Muncie after my display of power. "Hire me? For what? To break bonds?"

"When necessary, yes. To sense them as well, since I know that's also part of your blessing. But, more than that, I'd like to make sure that you don't use that ability against my people."

"So you're going to pay me *not* to use my 'gift'?"

"Mm. In a way."

There's got to be a catch. Being paid to act like I'm not a Luna-touched female? That's the freaking dream.

"Anything else?"

"Since you mention it," Roman begins, even as I want to say: *I knew it*, "I have another offer for you."

"Okay."

"I'm sure you know that vampires prefer the night.

Me? I'm old enough that I rarely sleep, but that's not the case for all of us. Our doors are open twenty-four hours a day for every citizen of Muncie. But because I can't hire just anyone to serve as a receptionist for me, I tend to struggle to find a vampire who will willingly take the dayshift. Did you see the vampire at the lobby desk?"

I nod.

"That's Leigh. She's doing the daylight hours temporarily as a favor to her mate. Eventually, she'll either take over at night or take on a patrol. You're a shifter. You're diurnal. I think you'd be perfect for the job."

And I'll be close enough that he can keep his eye on me. A shifter who can snap even a vampire's blood bond even though he acts as if he doesn't want me to? I'm just as valuable to Roman as I was to the Wicked Wolf.

On the plus side, I don't sense even a hint of interest coming from the cool vampire. Sure, he doesn't have a bond of his own, but my instincts tell me that, unlike the Alpha, he isn't going to try to convince me to join with him permanently.

Nope. He just wants to hire me.

And I need money way more than I need a mate.

"It won't be a difficult job. Answer calls, keep my schedule, do my filing. Keep out any unwanted visitors. Hardly taxing, and I'll pay you well for your time."

Steepling his fingers, Roman leans back in his chair. "What do you think?"

I think that I would be an idiot to refuse.

I'm used to those in authority wanting to warp my "gift" for themselves. Even before I developed the ability to break bonds—when my gift became my "gift", or sometimes *curse*—my Alpha used the way I could dampen scents to his advantage. I was happy to let him because it meant I was serving the pack. I was useful.

Needed.

If the vampire wants to hire me as a receptionist while really keeping an eye on me and my Luna-touched wolf, that's fine with me. I woke up this morning looking for a job. Charlie's was a bust, but this might just be a better fit for me after all.

"When can I start?"

THE SECOND I EXIT THE CADRE'S BUILDING, I PULL MY phone out of my pocket. There hadn't been time when Dominic told me that Roman wanted to see me, but since I don't have my first shift until tomorrow morning, I can call Gem now.

And after what went down in Roman's office, I really need to.

It takes her a couple of rings before she answers.

When she does, she squeals through the phone, "You got the job!"

"That bartending gig? Uh, no. I actually didn't."

"What?" Her excitement for me turns into a straight demand. "Why the hell not?"

Good question. "I don't know, but it's okay. I got *a* job."

"You did? That's great! I'm happy for you, Elizabeth. So... where are you working? What are you doing?"

"Thanks. As for what my new job is... that's actually part of the reason why I'm calling." Over the phone, it's so much easier to go against my wolf's instincts when it comes to the female alpha. I probably wouldn't dare ask her in person, but with miles between us, I manage to spit out, "Did you tell anyone in Muncie about my abilities? My... 'gift'?"

My *curse*?

She doesn't hesitate to answer. "Yeah. Remember? I said I might need to use that to convince Roman to let you stay. You said that was okay. Why?"

She's right. I did give her permission. From how she described Roman, he made every decision with the safety of his people in mind. But he wasn't heartless. Gem thought telling him that I was on the run from the Wicked Wolf of the West would be enough, but if he decided he didn't want my trouble following me into the city, my abilities were supposed to be her trump card.

I guess she had to use it.

"No reason. Just wanted to make sure that it didn't get any further than the leader of the Cadre."

"And let my sperm donor figure out that you settled down at the foot of Accalia? No fucking way. We still don't have any idea where he's hiding out, but if he learns that you're on the East Coast and we're practically neighbors, you know he won't be able to resist making a move. And, as much as I hate to admit it, even Ryker agrees that we're better off gunning for him instead of letting him attack us again."

She isn't wrong.

Just then, the same old familiar guilt starts to claw away at my insides. I'm not just risking my safety by settling down in one place, I'm also risking Gem's—and everyone who lives in Muncie.

Including my fated mate.

"Thanks for that. I just wanted to check. But, uh, I… I have to go now. I'll call you later. Okay?"

As an alpha, her senses are incredibly keen. Just like how I can resist her dominance, she can't catch my scent through the phone, but she doesn't need to. She immediately can tell that something is off by the tone of my voice.

"Is everything alright?"

"Uh. Yeah. Of course."

Gem's senses are keen, and I've always been a terrible liar.

"In that case, we should celebrate. Come to dinner. Here, in Accalia. I'd come down to Muncie, but... yeah. It's probably better if you come up here."

Where the phone won't make it difficult for her to use her dominance against me. I can't blame her for her tactics, either.

After all, she *is* an alpha.

"I start my new job tomorrow," I tell her. "Once I know what my schedule is, I'll make time to visit."

"You better. Or else I'm going to hunt you down and drag you up here so we can really chat."

I know Gemma well enough by now to tell that she's mostly teasing. Tell that to my submissive wolf. Even through the phone, she reacts to Gem's threat.

"I will. Promise."

The next morning, I wake up early, ready to start my new job.

Roman has me working at the front desk in the Cadre building's lobby from ten in the morning until six in the evening, Monday through Friday. If he needs me for any other reason, he has my phone number, making it clear that I'm expected to answer any call.

He doesn't give me his. I didn't expect him to.

My phone is basically a burner I bought for cheap right before I decided to visit Muncie. For now, I only have one number stored: Gem's. It rarely rings, so I'll know immediately if the call is coming from Roman. I'm fine with that.

Starting work as a receptionist?

That's a little more nerve-wracking.

I show up a good fifteen minutes early, lingering in the lobby when I see that two unfamiliar vampires are sitting behind the desk. They must be third shift; I'm considered first. I think about introducing myself before quietly moving to one corner of the lobby, waiting until the minutes pass and it's ten o'clock.

At two minutes before, a pair of female vampires glide into the lobby together. The one on the left is Black, her dark vampiric skin gleaming beneath the lights. She has her black hair styled in box braids that fall down her back; her light eyes are the closest to gold I've seen on a vampire.

I recognize her. She's Leigh, the vampire who was sitting behind the desk yesterday afternoon.

The one on the right is about an inch taller than her companion, with bright red hair, shockingly white skin, and a spattering of freckles over her nose. Her eyes are closer to green, though still with the tell-tale lightness that marks her as a vampire.

They're holding hands as they enter, and before they go their separate ways, they kiss.

Obviously. Even from my hidden corner, I could sense the solid bond stretching between them.

While the redhead disappears down the hall, Leigh unerringly tracks me down, a smile highlighting just how beautiful she is.

"Hello. I'm Leigh," she says, introducing herself even though I already knew that. "In case you're curious, the gorgeous redhead going up to check in with Roman? That's my beloved. Tamera. And you're—"

"I'm Elizabeth."

"I thought so." She scrunches her nose, then gives me an apologetic expression when she realizes what she had done. "Sorry, but I also thought you were supposed to be a wolf. Roman told me I'd be showing you what I do, but I definitely remember him telling me that you're a shifter."

"I am. Does that bother you?"

"Me? Nah. Maybe if I caught you when I was thirsty..." At the look on my face, she laughs, then quickly says, "I'm just kidding."

I'm pretty sure she's not.

Glancing over her shoulder, she sees the two other vampires getting up from their seats. "Looks like it's time to switch shifts. Come on. Let me show you what I do when I first arrive."

And that's the end of us discussing that I'm a shifter. Seems as if, now that Roman's hired me, I'm Cadre. In a Fang City, that's all that matters.

The job, I decide, is kind of basic even if there's a lot to learn; makes sense, since Roman didn't hire me for my secretarial skills. Leigh is kind and patient with me. She's also friendlier than I expected any vampire to be, and before long I start to feel a little more comfortable sitting next to her as she shows me how to work the computer and answer phones.

Then, when the mail delivery comes, she even shows me how to go through it.

It arrives in a massive cart since we're responsible for all of the mail in the whole of the Cadre building. As the daytime receptionists, this is one of our main jobs. I don't mind. It's something to keep me busy.

Until I reach inside the mail bin and feel a jolt of electricity when I brush against one particular package.

Leigh was sorting mail on a folding table she set out for just that purpose. "You alright?"

I nod even as I drag that package out from under all of the others. As soon as it's free from the pile, an enticing scent wafts up from the cardboard box.

My first instinct is that it smells of *hope*. My wolf—who's been dozing as soon as she realized that Leigh is no threat to us—perks her head up, snout snuffling as she takes the scent into her as well.

What the—

It's addressed to *me*.

Looking over my shoulder, Leigh notices it the

same time as I do. Her nostrils flare, picking up the same scent as I did. I don't know what it smells like to her, but she's quicker than I am.

She obviously recognizes it, too.

"A package from Aleksander Filan? And it's addressed to you?"

"It looks that way," I say weakly.

Because that *is* Aleks's scent. And instead of pinpointing it immediately, my first reaction was to think of hope.

Yeah... that can't be good.

Leigh's expression turns curious. "You know him? He's pretty high up in the Cadre. I thought you just started today?"

"I did." I'm still staring at the cardboard box. Giving my head a clearing shake, I add, "And I don't know him. Not really. I mean, I've heard of him, but I've never met him."

Every last part of that is true. I just kind of, sort of neglect to mention that my goddess won't give up on the idea that the mysterious vampire is my fated mate.

And now he's sent me a package.

I open the box at Leigh's urging, just as curious as she is.

It's... a box of teabags?

Why would Aleks send me teabags?

I don't know. There's no doubt that it's meant for

me—Elizabeth Howell is definitely printed on the label—but I... I don't understand.

As far as I know, he has no clue who I am.

And now he's sent me *tea*?

Leigh uses the pen in her hand to point at the package I'm still holding. "That's the good stuff, too."

"Is it?" I ask vaguely, setting it down, pushing it away from me. "I wouldn't know. I don't drink tea."

"Really? Then why did Aleksander send you some to the Cadre building?"

That is a very good question. Too bad I have no idea how I'm supposed to get an answer to it.

So I shrug, and hope that's the end of it—and it is if only because, suddenly, the phone rings.

Leigh answers it and, after a quick exchange, she says, "Roman would like to speak to you."

When I reach for the phone, she shakes her head before dropping the office phone back into its cradle. "I forgot you're new here. When Roman wants to talk to you, he means in person. He wants you to go up to his office."

Okay, then.

IT'S LIKE DÉJÀ VU. ME, STANDING IN THE MIDDLE OF Roman's office. The powerful vampire giving me a searching look while I wonder what part of me he's scrutinizing now.

After a few minutes when I contemplate throwing myself out of the freaking window, he nods, then gestures for me to take a seat.

Taking a twenty-one-story nosedive seems pretty tempting when the alternative is sitting with barely a few feet separating me from the leader of the Cadre. But I do because, as big of a coward as I am, I'm a wolf. The drive to survive is almost as undeniable as the one to mate.

Then again, I have made it five months rejecting *that* urge...

I sit, folding my hands primly in my lap. Hey. It's the only way to hide how much they're shaking.

"How are you liking your work so far?"

"It's going well," I tell him honestly. "Leigh has been very helpful."

"Good to hear that. So you'll be staying on then?"

I hadn't realized today was a trial. Trying to calm my racing heart, I say, "I'd like to. If you'll let me."

"I think that will be for the best," Roman agrees. "But now that you're part of the Cadre, I'm as responsible for you as any of my people. Here. I want you to have this."

His hand is folded in a fist. When he gestures for me to come closer and offer him mine, I do. He opens his fingers, dropping a golden chain into my waiting palm.

Attached to the center of the chain is a bright, white vampire fang.

I marvel down at it. It absolutely hums with power. "What is this?"

"Dominic told me about the fangs you carried here yesterday. My people won't respect any that weren't freely given. But this one? They will."

"How is this any different than the ones I collected from my old pack?" I wonder, peeking up at him again, making sure he knows that that was exactly where I got those other fangs from.

Roman curls his lip, showing off an even white smile—and a missing fang.

Oh, boy. That explains the power I felt. "This is yours."

"You work for me, Elizabeth. This is a symbol of protection. No more, no less. But I do insist that you wear it while you live within my borders."

Make him explain... that's what Gem told me, but she meant Aleks.

I think she'd understand why I'm too terrified to ask the leader of the Cadre why he's giving me one of his fangs.

"Wear it over your heart. I've hung it on a golden chain since I know silver bothers shifters as much as it does my kind. No vampire should give you any trouble within the city if you do."

You know what? Maybe this is one of the benefits he mentioned when he offered me the job.

Protection and a paycheck? I'll take it.

Something tells me that I don't have a choice, either.

"Thank you."

"Don't thank me, Elizabeth. Never forget, I only do what's best for my city. For my city, and for those loyal to me. Be one of them, and you have nothing to fear. But betray me?"

Roman's strange eyes flash in warning.

I gulp.

He nods. "Then I trust we understand each other."

More than he ever knows. "Yes."

"Good."

CHAPTER 5

When Gem pulls open the door to the cabin she shares with her mate up in Accalia, the first thing she does is give the fang necklace I'm wearing a side-eye. Gesturing for me to step inside, she closes the door, then spins on me.

She points. "That's not Aleks's."

I don't even ask how she can tell the difference. Alphas... they're wired differently than most shifters. Their senses are more keen, including their eyes and their noses, and they sense things the rest of us don't. Lies, for example. Bad intentions. In order to be the lead protector for a pack, they need those skills. It doesn't surprise me at all that she can look at one fang and know it's not the same as another.

"No. It's not. And before you ask, I did make it a point to find out what it means when a vampire offers an unmated female one of his fangs. That's not the case here. He told me it's not a proposal, but for protection instead."

"He?"

"Yeah. Roman."

Gem's eyebrows shoot sky-high. "Roman? Roman Zakharov?"

"Yeah. I work for him now. Three days so far, and it's been going great."

"Hang on... you *what*?"

The way her voice went all high like that... my wolf is suddenly contemplating a quick retreat. "I told you I got a job—"

"Yeah," she says, cutting me off. "It was supposed to be at Charlie's. I thought you were gonna work behind the bar like I used to until you told me he didn't hire you. And now the cagey bastard is ignoring my calls."

"I'm sorry." What else can I say?

"Don't worry about it. I'll get to the bottom of it eventually. But you working for Zakharov? Let's go sit down in the living room. I think I'm going to want to be sitting down to hear this one."

Gem leads me away from the promise of a quick escape, bringing me to a living room full of alpha pheromones. My wolf hesitates in the doorway, yipping when she realizes that Ryker Wolfson is sitting in one of the armchairs, a map sprawled across his lap. He has a red marker clutched in his right hand, jotting notes on the paper as he consults something on his phone.

Sidling around me, Gem says, "You don't have to worry about him. Ryker's all bark, no bite."

As if to prove that he's not as absorbed in his work as it appears, Ryker lifts his head, snapping his teeth at us.

I jump, and Gem rolls her eyes. "Ignore him. He's just pissy that he can't have my undivided attention today. As if I can ever compete with that damn map of his."

"Love you, too, sweetheart," Ryker calls out, already adding another note to the map's corner.

He means it. I'm pretty sure that, even without my "gift", I would be able to tell just how much he cares for Gem. It's in the way he angles his body in the seat, always keeping her centered, and in the way he sneaks peeks at her as she shoots him her middle finger before bounding over to take a seat on the couch. That's pure affection mingled with outright lust when he takes her flipping the bird literally.

My cheeks heat up as his dark gold eyes turn molten. He's probably already imagining it, and I'm the only thing keeping his fantasies from being acted out.

"I can always come back another night," I offer. "If I'm interrupting anything."

Gem pats the open seat next to her on the couch. "You're not interrupting anything. We had plans first, and I'll make it up to him later." The pheromones in the room thicken so quickly, I know exactly how she'll be doing just that. "Forget him, Elizabeth. I want to hear all about you and Roman?"

Ryker's head jerks up. "What was that?"

"There is no me and Roman," I say quickly. "He's my boss. That's all. Remember how I asked if you told him that I was Luna-touched? That I could break bonds?"

"You said I could. I needed some reason why you'd prefer living with vamps instead of up here with us, and telling him about you being Luna-touched did the trick."

"I know. But that's exactly it. He asked me to prove it, and when I did, he wants to make sure that I only use it at his request. He gave me a job as his secretary, but we both know that it's my 'gift' that makes me valuable to him."

"It also makes you a security risk," Gem points out. "If other supes know about it, they might come after you in Muncie."

I nod. That's also very true.

Though I know all three of us are thinking it, no one mentions Wicked Wolf Walker. He kept me close for two years because of what I could do. Odds of him coming back from me are pretty high. Unlike

Gem, I would never challenge him, and we all know it.

"You want a guard? Take one of mine. I have *three*."

"That's okay." I pat Roman's fang. "This is enough for me, I think."

"No. Please. I mean it." If I didn't know any better, I'd think Gem was pleading with me. "Take at least one. What about Jace? He's cute."

Ryker growls low in his chest.

"Something wrong?" she tosses behind her easily to her mate.

"I'll say. Please don't make me challenge my Beta again, sweetheart. We finally got a new one. It would be a shame to put Jace down just because you think he's cute."

I almost choke on my laugh. I can't help it. It's such... such an *Alpha* thing to say, that any awkward tension in the room slips away with Ryker's threat.

"You've got nothing to worry about, Ryker." Gem grins before blowing a kiss over at him. "Jace is cute. You, my mate, are fucking sexy as hell."

Ryker is slightly mollified by that. "Better. But stop trying to get rid of your guards. Duke is an exception. You know the other three won't give up on you."

"Yeah, yeah." Turning her back to him again, missing the way his eyes follow her every move, she leans into me. "Speaking of mates... how are things with Aleks?"

I exhale. As much as I wanted to see Gem, to talk to another shifter female... I just can't talk to her about Aleks. Mainly because there's nothing really I can say about him, but also because of their history.

For a year, Aleks courted her, trying to convince her to be his mate. He gave her his necklace, only it wasn't just for protection; he had claimed her as his intended. She never really gave his pursuit any thought since she's always known that Ryker Wolfson was meant to be her mate, but Aleks tried to get her to change her mind all the way up until the week of her Luna Ceremony, when Ryker and Gem finalized their mate bond.

She told me all of this when I finally agreed to stay in her townhouse in Muncie. She wanted to be honest so she wasn't going to hide her past with Aleks. She was his roommate, nothing more, but in case it got out, she was letting me know before I ran into Aleks again.

At first, I thought she was mentioning Aleks because she knew he lived there, and that he would want revenge for how the Wicked Wolf treated him in the district. Before long, I realized that she sensed that I felt something toward the vampire.

When she asked, I told her I had no idea what she was talking about, and she called me out on it. I thought it was because I'm a crappy liar. Nope. Like I can sense bonds, she can sense lies.

So I folded. I told her that the Luna said that Aleks was meant to be mine.

Luckily, she promised she wouldn't interfere. If I wanted to stay away from Aleks, that was fine. And since the most the vampire did was pace outside of the townhouse, I left it at that.

Hey. I can take a hint. If he feels anything toward me, he's pretending he can't. I'm perfectly okay with it.

See? I really am such an awful liar. I can't even lie to myself.

"How's Aleks? Same as before," I tell her. "I saw him the other day, but he didn't even seem to notice me."

It was so quick. Though I pretended not to notice at the time, no denying he was walking out of the bar right as I was walking out of the back room following the disastrous interview. I was flagged down by Dominic, and by the time I followed him onto the street, Aleks was already long gone.

"He will," she says firmly. "You might not want him to, but he will sooner or later. But that's okay. I got something for you for when he does."

"You... you do?"

"Yup." Gem jumps up, holding her hands out. "Don't move. I'll go get it for you."

"Um. Okay."

I knew she was inhumanly fast. Even fast for a shifter, too. After the dinner where she discovered that Walker regarded me as his pet, when he was bragging about my "gift", she turned on me. One minute we were walking into my cabin, the next she had her claws centimeters from my throat. I never even saw her move.

Now, she dashes from the room. Ryker's dark gold eyes are drawn to her ass as she goes. He gives his head a shake, almost like he'd been in a trance, then glances over at me and shrugs, his unabashed smile turning the stoic Alpha into a ruggedly handsome male.

My heart skips a beat. No wonder Gem was willing to hold onto her mate with both paws. If I had a male who looked at me like he does Gem, I'd never want to let him go, either.

She's back in a flash, holding something out to me. "Here you go."

It's a book. Flipping it over so that I can see the title, I give her a quizzical look. "A Polish dictionary?"

"Polish to English," she corrects. "Trust me. You're going to need it."

If she says so.

Roman's fang keeps me protected in the Fang City. Ryker and Gem have given me permission to visit pack territory. Theoretically, I should be in no danger on my way back from my visit to the Mountainside Pack.

In between Accalia and Muncie, there's a dirt road that's about twenty feet wide. It's a road that leads into the mountains, as well as out of the vampire's territory; the next city over is straight-out human, just past the River Run Pack's wooded land. It's considered the official border between two powerful supe communities, a kind of no man's land.

Fittingly, that's where the female shifter is waiting for me.

It's my fault, too. I've grown so used to being able to walk around without looking over my shoulder since I arrived in Muncie that I never thought twice about leaving it. I forgot that Roman's fang is just a weird fashion choice outside of the Cadre-run city, or that I have a massive target on my back.

It's been seven years since I met her last. Peyton Slate, the former mate to the Beta of the Oak Valley Pack.

I can't believe this is happening—though I probably shouldn't be surprised. She'd promised revenge on me like so many others, and now that I'm free again, she didn't waste that much time coming after me.

Damn it. I let my guard down. My wolf is up inside of my chest, her ears folded back against her skull. I can feel my eyes darken from silver to black, a mixture of fear and disgust.

She's not only wearing her scent on her skin.

He's here. I don't know where, his scent apart from the way it mingles with hers is faint, but it's near.

Walker.

Peyton, I can handle. She's a delta, so not much more powerful than me, and her broken bond is a weakness I can exploit if I have to. But Peyton *and* the Wicked Wolf?

I'm fucking doomed.

With a nasty look on her face, Peyton runs her claws through the length of her pitch-black hair. It's styled in loose curls that frame her face, highlighting the cruel twist to her mouth, her patrician nose, and her eyes.

Her eyes...

They used to be a bright shifter gold. Since the last time I've seen her, they've *changed*. Like the malice tucked in her smile, they're darker. Angrier. More of a burnt yellow than gold, they promise retribution.

Her lips curve.

My stomach plummets. "What are you doing here?" There's no doubt in my mind that she was waiting for me in particular. "What do you want from me, Peyton?"

"Isn't it obvious? You took my mate from me. It's only fair I take yours from you."

UP UNTIL I WAS EIGHTEEN, THERE WERE ONLY TWO CLUES that I, like the rest of my mother's line, had been touched by the Luna: my silver eyes, and how I didn't quite fit into our pack because I was *other*.

Just because I was out of the hierarchy, though, that didn't mean I was an outcast. Far from it. My mother was revered for her connection to our goddess, and my fellow packmates treated me the same way. Around puberty, I developed the ability to cover my scent and those who were around me. It was a huge advantage when it came to hunting, and I truly considered it to be a gift.

And then, a couple of weeks after I came of age, I accidentally touched my Alpha's mate.

Their bond broke instantly.

I hadn't known I could do that. The weeks leading up to that birthday, I had started to sense the bonds in my packmates. I could tell how they were related to each other, who was a fated match, and who was chosen. The nuances came later—sensing the promise of a bond, or when one was shaky—but I had no idea that a simple brush of my hand could snap a mate bond in half.

There had to be doubt. One of them had to have been looking for a way out, unhappy in their mating. Of course, I didn't know that at the time.

All I knew was that I destroyed my Alpha.

He'd protected me and my family from anyone outside of our pack learning the truth of our line, and how did I repay him? By separating him from his fated mate forever. The Luna refused to bless their mating a second time.

And it was all my fault.

I ran. With nothing except the clothes on my back, I ran.

Those early days, I was little more than a scavenger. I never went fully feral, though it was close. I'm not exactly proud to say that I did whatever I could to survive. After abandoning my pack, I shied away from shifters; turning to other supes for help never occurred to me. I fell in with the humans, tucking my wolf down deep as I tried desperately to pass among them.

I stole. I slept with males if I got some food or money out of it. When I stumbled upon unclaimed land, I spent days in my fur, always being run off by either other lone wolves or real predatory animals who sensed the two-legged side of me.

And then, a few months into my new life, I stumbled upon a traveling carnival.

I'd learned it was better to hide among humans, especially those who had no idea that supes existed. Explaining away my silver eyes as colored contacts, they didn't have the nose or the instinct to know I was different; those who intuitively sensed my wolf gave me a wide berth. At the carnival, I was looking for the safety of the crowd and the chance to steal some food, and that was all.

I found something better.

A beautiful human female with eyes as deep blue as the sea was sitting in a simple stall, a deck of weathered yet intricately illustrated tarot cards set in front of her. Over her head, there was a sign. It had the stereotypical crystal ball painted on it, and it read:

Madame Zoe
Palm readings $5
Tarot readings $10

She picked me out of the crowd. When I murmured that I had no money to pay for any kind of reading, she pulled a single card for me for free.
Wheel of Fortune.
With a secretive smile, she pulled another.
The Moon.
It was nighttime. The carnival was bright with neons and spotlights, my wolf laying her head on her paw to avoid the sights and the sounds. The air smelled of fried foods and the musty stink when too many humans were together, and still I sensed something... intoxicating about the fortune-teller.

Crooking her finger, she beckoned me closer. Then, without a word, she reached below her table, grabbing a wooden box. Her voice had a thick accent I couldn't quite place, when she said, "For you. Use them well."

She gave me my deck of tarot cards that night, as well as a change in my fortune.

Just like her cards said.

From that moment on, I did exactly as she said. Instead of frequenting carnivals, I set up a lopsided tray table on city street corners, telling fortunes until it became second nature. I never earned enough to be considered comfortable, and life as a lone wolf meant I could never settle down for long, but it was better than it used to be.

Then, four years later, I met a shifter in the city I was living in and, for the first time, I didn't run. Then, when Kyle Ridgewood tracked me down despite me hiding my scent, I thought: *This is it.*

This could be *fate*.

I couldn't have been more wrong.

I was twenty-two, my wolf aching for some sense of community; love and touch, too. I'd been alone for so long, and when I first looked into his golden eyes, I felt the echo of a bond reaching toward me.

Back then, I didn't understand my curse as much as I do now. I didn't know the difference between a possible bond and one that had been finalized. I just saw a handsome male, felt a bond brush against me, and fell head over heels.

I fell into his bed, too. For weeks, I acted as if I was Kyle's mate; he even told me I was a member of the Oak Valley Pack—his pack—even though I never left the city. I ate his food, cooked him meals, and mated him any time I had the chance. He had been visiting the city I was living in for pack business that fateful day, and though he came back to see me every weekend after that, I loved the idea of eventually moving to stay with him in Oak Valley.

He promised to bring me back to live with him in the protected woods of his pack eventually, giving me a place where I could finally belong. All I needed to do was be patient while he explained to his Alpha that he wanted to choose a lone wolf—and a recent packmate —for his.

I'm not like Gem. I can't tell instinctively when someone is lying to me. I could guess, but I wouldn't know for sure until presented with the proof.

Like, oh, his furious mate showing up on my doorstep, ready to challenge me for the right to call Kyle hers.

Because *surprise*. Kyle neglected to mention over the months we were together that he already had a bonded mate. Peyton was actually his *fated* mate, and his Alpha pushed him to claim her even though he was reckless and wild and didn't want to settle down. Most bonded shifters were incredibly loyal to their mates once they take them; as Kyle and the Wicked Wolf prove, though, it's not *all* shifters. Though he was Peyton's in name, he mated available females whenever he wanted to.

And then he set his eyes on me, and I inadvertently gave him two things he desired desperately: his freedom from an unwanted bond and a willing pussy with no real strings attached. The first time I slept with him, I broke the thread tying him to Peyton. It never occurred to me that he was already taken. Sure, he had a white scar on his shoulder, but he explained it away as a shifter tattoo and not a mating mark.

So what if I knew that mating marks were white and shifter tattoos were more a silvery gray? I wanted so badly to be loved that I overlooked all the warning signs—until Peyton showed up, ready and willing to claw my guts out for getting between her and Kyle.

I managed to avoid that by siccing the furious female on her former mate. Kyle was lying in my bed, sated and drowsy after another round of vigorous mating when she unexpectedly appeared. My scent on his skin had Peyton nearly frothing at the mouth. As she charged into the room, I grabbed my deck of cards, my purse, and the spare pair of flip-flops I kept by the door, and I was gone. He lied to me, making me promises he couldn't keep. Bitter at his betrayal, me and my wolf both agreed he deserved whatever his spurned mate was going to dish out.

Only Peyton didn't do anything too terrible. I'd heard rumors that, for a while, she tried to pretend she still had a mate bond with Kyle after she dragged him back to pack territory. When that didn't work, she fled the Oak Valley Pack on her own, leaving Kyle free to be the manwhore that he was.

Now, seven years later, she's found me. But, unlike then, she's not threatening to gut me.

No. She just wants to take my fated mate.

You know what? Go right ahead, Peyton.

Aleks isn't mine. He'll never be mine, either.

"You're wasting your time," I tell her. "I don't have a mate."

It's the truth. So why does my wolf bare her teeth when Peyton's lips curve in a wicked smile?

"That so?"

"Yeah."

Peyton snorts. "You were a shit liar back then, too, Howell. Telling me you had no idea that Kyle was mine. Now you expect me to believe that you don't know that you're someone's intended?"

"I don't care what you believe," I say, bravado filling my voice. "If you want to blame anyone, blame him. Blame Kyle. He courted me. He initiated mating with me. He touched me. Your bond broke because he never wanted it."

"You're still trying to lie. Do it again and I'll go for your vocal cords, you silver-eyed freak."

I'm not a liar when it comes to this. I'm *not*.

"Stop this, Peyton."

"No. You think you're so much better than me because of the Luna. You're not. And I look forward to fucking your mate whenever I want." Lifting up her hand, Peyton flexes her fingers, showing off her sharpened claws. "Carving up his back. Marking him again and again until his flesh is nothing but bloody pulp. Maybe then you'll know that some things are sacred." She scoffs. "Maybe then you'll understand what you took from me."

A male who preferred getting his dick wet over being loyal to his fated mate. That's what I took from her, but if Peyton is still holding a grudge after seven years, there's nothing I can say now that will change her mind.

I'm not always liar, but I'm definitely not a fighter. Not really. I never have been. But before the Luna's touch changed my life, I was a maternal she-wolf. I adored watching over the pups, and even if they weren't mine, they were pack. I'm not a fighter, but I would go feral to protect them.

When Peyton threatens Aleks, it doesn't matter that I've spent weeks—*months*—rejecting what the Luna tells me constantly. He's meant to be mine, even if I can't have him. I won't let her hurt him, especially before I can figure out what *he* thinks of *me*.

My silver eyes shift to black as my claws lengthen, matching Peyton's. "No. You won't."

"Who's gonna stop me, freak?"

"I am."

"Go right ahead," dares Peyton. "Give me your best shot."

Our gazes are locked. This is a challenge, in more

ways than one. The stakes are higher than they were when she stepped out of the trees marking the boundary of the dirt road, and I know that if our wolves start fighting, only one of us will walk away.

And that's when a voice calls out to me.

"Elizabeth? Is that you?"

CHAPTER 6

If I look over my shoulder, I'll break the stare with Peyton. Unacceptable. She'll take it as me losing our little challenge, and I can't have that.

Luckily, I don't need to look behind me to know who has just joined us.

Dominic.

I exhale in relief. *Saved by the vampire.*

I would've fought Peyton if I had to. I'm just super glad that I don't.

"This isn't over," she sneers, the first one to look away as her dark yellow eyes lock on something over my shoulder. "I have plans for you. One way or another, you'll pay for what you did to me. To us. Your precious parasites might've saved you tonight, but don't get used to it."

Then, with a snap of her human teeth, she shifts. A

sleek grey wolf takes the place of the black-haired female. Growling low, her ears flat against her skull, Peyton's wolf kicks some snow up at me before loping away just as Dominic approaches me from behind.

Together, we watch the wolf disappear into the distance.

"Friend of yours?" he asks.

Not even a little. "She's a shifter," I tell him needlessly. The pile of torn clothes by my feet, plus the wolf prints hightailing it down the stretch of dirt road are a couple of big, honking clues what type of female Peyton is.

Dominic frowns. "You didn't invite her into the city, did you? I know Roman has approved your stay, and the Mountainside Alpha's mate can still visit, but that's it. No other shifters."

I shake my head. "No. Actually, I was just telling her she had to go."

"You should probably head home, too. We patrol the borders for a reason. It's not always safe out here."

He doesn't know the half of it. If Dominic hadn't come over to check up on me, I don't know what Peyton would've done—or me, for that matter.

One thing for sure: I wouldn't have liked it.

Satisfied that he got his point across, Dominic says, "Allez. Come on. I'll walk with you back a bit."

When he goes to take my elbow to steer me past the border that leads into Muncie, I move out of his reach. It's an instinctive gesture; I don't let anyone touch me if I can avoid it. I haven't accidentally severed a bond since Kyle. I've learned control. Learned how to use my curse instead of it using me. However, with Peyton's taunts and threats echoing in my ears, I can't be too careful.

I just removed an unwanted blood bonding from Dominic. I can already sense that a new one has taken its place. As shaky as I am right now, a simple brush against my skin might snap it.

"It's okay," I say, lying through my teeth. I'm not always a liar, but sometimes I *am*. "I'm okay. I wouldn't want to keep you from your patrol."

He frowns as if he can tell I'm completely full of it. "Does Roman know you left the city? I don't think he would approve."

My hand lifts to my chest, patting the fang nestled there. Peyton had thrown the fang a look of disgust, but in Muncie, it's basically my golden ticket. The fact that it's Roman Zakharov's token is supposed to be special, but I don't ever want his vampires to get the wrong idea. He was very clear: he traded his fang and his protection to have control of my abilities. That doesn't mean he can tell me what to do, right?

"I'm off duty. Roman can't tell me what to do when I'm off the clock."

"You've not been in the city long enough, cher. When you live in Muncie a little longer, you'll understand that the Cadre... and especially Roman... tells us all what to do. And we do it."

He pats me on the shoulder. I feel the hum of a secure bond through my shirt.

"Don't worry. You'll get used to it."

Honestly? I'm a low-ranked shifter. Following an established authority is kind of hard-wired into me and my wolf. It'll be easy to fall in line if I have to so that's not really what's weighing on me right now.

Fact is, Dominic's perfect timing saved me from a fight I'm not so sure I could've won. A regular delta female... I could take down one of those easily.

But a broken shifter with a jagged bond?

I don't think so.

Worse, Peyton will be back. I'm sure of it.

And I still haven't said two words to Aleksander Filan since I've been in Muncie.

ONCE I MADE IT BACK TO THE TOWNHOUSE, I CALLED Gem and let her know about my run-in with Peyton. I hesitate over whether or not I should tell her I sensed her father before deciding that she deserved to know.

It's okay. I recovered the hearing in my right ear about twenty minutes after her furious curse nearly blew out my eardrum, and at least she's on her guard now, too. Her overprotective mate is probably going to give her a hard time whenever she leaves their cabin for a while, but I couldn't *not* tell her after everything she's done for me so far.

The next morning, I walk to work, a little less confident than I was the day before. I have Roman's fang, and Gem assured me that the Cadre's constant patrols should keep Peyton and Walker out. When I doubt that, I remember how Dominic popped up so suddenly. With as many patrollers as Roman employs, odds are if he hadn't, someone else would've.

No one bothers me the entire walk from the townhouse to the Cadre building in the center of the city. Taking that as a good sign, I walk into the lobby, shrug off the coat I wear to blend in with the humans in Muncie, and fold it up.

Leigh is already sitting behind the counter. She's talking to a tall, leggy blonde whose forearms are resting on the countertop. I murmur a quick 'good morning' to her as I stow my coat and my purse on one of the shelves below our shared desk.

As I do, I hear someone click their tongue. Glancing up, I see it's the blonde. With her flawless features, her pale eyes, and her vaguely judgmental expression, I pin her as another vampire.

"Oh," she says. "Who is this? Let me guess. It's Aleksander's new puppy."

I freeze, like a deer in headlights.

What does she know?

Better questions: *how* does she know?

"Gretchen. Be nice."

"What? You're the one who told me about the box of teabags and—"

With a casual gesture that's somehow still incredibly obvious, Leigh brushes her hands over her impressive chest.

Gretchen immediately looks at mine.

"Oh."

"Uh-huh."

Her skin is already alabaster, but she goes impossibly paler. Like, so pale I can almost see through her. Muttering something under her breath, she gives me an incredibly fake smile. "Let's forget what I just said, okay? Hello. I'm Gretchen, and you are?"

...so incredibly impressed that me wearing Roman's fang just knocked the mean girl out of her.

"Elizabeth."

Her gaze looks me up and down. "She's not as mangy as the last one, is she, Leigh? I suppose, if Roman was gonna mark one, she'll do."

Okay. Maybe not *all* of the mean girl.

Next to me, Leigh looks like she wants to get up and slap some duct tape over Gretchen's mouth.

Huh. I now understand why Gem calls the trio of Gretchen, Tamera, and Leigh the Nightmare Trio; she'd groaned when I admitted that I worked with Leigh, and met Tamera. I thought Gem was being kind of catty since Tamera seems friendly enough and Leigh's been good to me so far, but now that I've met their ringleader?

I get it. I do.

She's not all that malicious, though. I don't know. Maybe it's because I spent the last ten years mainly living among humans, but if that's the worst that Gretchen is going to dish out? I can take it.

I smile at her, and hers wavers. "I'm glad to meet you. I've heard so much about you already."

"All good things, I expect."

"The best."

Gretchen fluffs her hair. "As it should be. Leigh loves me."

"I do," Leigh mutters on a sigh, as if she can't believe that she does. "Almost as much as my beloved. And I love it when you stop by, Gretch, but is there anything you need? Because I've got a lot of training to do with Elizabeth and—"

"I hope you're not being a distraction, Gretchen. If you're bored, perhaps you'd like to join Tamera and Leigh in the Cadre."

Aleks.

As his lightly accented voice washes over us, Gretchen spins around, moving just enough that I can't miss him.

My breath catches in my throat. He was standing

right behind Gretchen, and her vampire aura covered him until he announced his presence like that.

Suddenly, it's all I can do not to notice that *he's right there*. Even though the counter is between us, this is the closest I've been to him since that night in the Wolf District.

He's just as beautiful as I remember. More, really, when you factor in his fresh haircut, his clean-shaven cheeks, and a perfectly fitted sweater that doesn't have a single bullet hole in it.

My heart skips a beat. I'm pretty sure every supe in the building noticed, too.

"Join the Cadre? Actually spend my days working when I can be sleeping? No, thanks, Aleksander," Gretchen tells him, hurriedly stepping further away from the counter. I have half a mind to beg her to stay. "I was just saying hello to Leigh before I turned in. I've done that, now I'll be on my way."

She's gone in an instant, leaving me torn between gaping after her—or gawking at the male who's moved directly in front of me.

Leigh looks as surprised to see him as I do. "Aleksander. How can we help you?"

He's staring at me—but not just *me*. Unless I'm imagining it, his pale eyes are locked on my chest. As if he can see right through my shirt, I know he's sensing Roman's fang hanging around my neck just like Gretchen had. He doesn't seem to react to it one way or another, and I'm not sure how to feel about that.

But—and, again, unless I'm imagining it—he does seem to be waiting for me to acknowledge him. If that's so, he's going to be waiting a long, long time.

Aleks takes a breath, about to speak.

I tense. It's instinctive.

What if he says something to me? Would he mention the box of teabags? Worse, will he say anything about California?

What about *bonds*?

Before I start to work myself up to a panic, I remind myself that I've never been officially introduced to him. I cling to that as my trembling hands shuffle through the pile of papers in front of me. Looking down at the pages, my eyes are unseeing as I strain to hear their pleasant conversation over the pounding of my heart.

Get it under control, Elizabeth.

The male vampire might just think I'm nervous because of him—and he wouldn't be wrong—but my co-worker would know for sure that something's up. I've worked alongside her for a few days so far and, until now, I've never been so close to losing my shit.

I blame the gorgeous vampire drumming his short yet neat nails against the top of the counter. I don't know. It's like we had an unspoken agreement to pretend the other didn't exist. He stalked me from outside of the townhouse, and I acted like I had no idea that he was standing there, looking up at my window, before disappearing into the shadows of the night and the softly fallen snow.

It's worked so far. Since I joined Leigh as one of Roman's secretaries, I thought that it would continue that way, the inexplicable box of teabags notwithstanding.

Guess not.

He opens his mouth. I try not to make it obvious that I'm listening, only relaxing when he says in his lightly accented and cultured voice, "I'm here to see Roman."

Leigh clicks on her mouse, pulling something up on her computer. "You're not on his schedule."

"No. But he'll see me."

Aleks must have some kind of pull around here. The first thing I was taught during training was that no one—absolutely *no one*—was allowed past the lobby if they weren't on Roman's schedule.

But, instead of telling Aleks that, Leigh types something, then nods. "Okay. It's right—"

"Yes. Thank you, Leigh. I know the way."

He strides down the hall, heading straight for the elevator. I can sense Leigh watching me closely, curiosity written all over her lovely face. When she starts to speak, I quickly cut her off, asking her a question about something written on the page I'm holding.

Thankfully, she doesn't push me on the subject of

Aleks. Returning to her role of trainer, she answers my question, then gestures for me to scoot closer so that she can show me how to view Roman's schedule on the computer.

I've barely learned how to open the program on my own when the reception desk's phone begins to buzz.

I'm not even a little surprised when Leigh reminds me again that the red light means it's coming from inside the Cadre building. Like Roman's office maybe?

She picks it up, and after a quick exchange, sets the receiver back down again.

With a slightly sympathetic expression, she turns to me. "Roman wants to see you."

Crap. From the moment Aleks disappeared behind the elevator's closed doors, I was afraid of something like that happening. Call it intuition—or my wolfish instinct—but I couldn't help but think that Fate decided I was taking my sweet time in regarding Aleks as my fated mate. If I wasn't going to go to him, maybe it was time my mate came to me.

Rising up from my seat, I just hope that he's already made a quick retreat himself by the time I climb all the stairs up to Roman's office.

He hasn't.

Like the first time I met him, Roman is seated behind

his desk. To his right, as far from the entrance as he can get, Aleks is watching with an unblinking gaze as I ease the door in, then slowly step into the opulent office.

I can feel the weight of his stare on me. Pretending I don't, I focus solely on my boss.

"You wanted to see me?"

"Ah, Elizabeth, yes." He waves at the pair of leather chairs across from his desk. "Please. Take a seat."

With Aleks leaning oh so casually against the far wall, I don't feel comfortable being the only one of us two sitting down. But what can I do?

I take the seat.

He gestures in Aleks's direction. "This is Aleksander Filan. He's one of my trusted patrollers. I hope you find that you can trust him as well."

He's supposed to be my mate. If I can't trust him, I have even bigger problems than I thought.

Roman doesn't know that, though. Neither does Aleks, I'm willing to bet. As far as they're aware, this is a simple introduction.

With a shy nod, purposely avoiding meeting his gaze, I say, "Hello."

Aleks nods. It's brisk and quick and almost standoffish.

My wolf whines inside of my chest. Lifting my hand, I rub between my boobs, trying to settle her.

Roman follows the motion. For a second, I pause,

misunderstanding his intent expression. A second later, I realize that he isn't watching my hand but, instead, his fang.

"You've kept it on. Good."

Of course I did. He told me I had to.

Thinking about how the blonde vampire reacted when she saw it, I murmur, "Thanks. It's worked so far."

"I'm glad. But that's exactly why I've called this meeting today. Forgive me, but I was... distracted when I gave it to you."

Oh. Reaching behind me to unclasp it, I ask, "Do you want it back?"

"No, no. Of course not. It's just... Aleks here has reminded me that a fang from a Cadre leader is different from others," Roman says. "It's a mark of favor. Of protection. Those who follow me—or those who fear me—will respect it. But"—his near colorless eyes are strikingly rimmed with red—"there are those in my city who won't. And they'll make you pay for wearing it."

So, in other words, I'm in the same situation I was in while I was still living in the Wolf District. He's marked me as his pet, and now there's a target on my back. Because of my tiny association with Roman, vampires will be gunning for my blood, just like Gem suspected.

Damn it! I took the fang so that this exact situation *wouldn't* happen.

And, okay. I'm still trying to deal with Peyton's unexpected appearance last night. With her threat hanging over my head, I already knew my time in the Fang City would be cut short. If she found me, it was only a matter of time before the Alpha did. The fact that she was near enough to him recently to wear his scent on her skin—which usually only happens after a mating—means that I'm already beginning to look over my shoulder again for that handsome face and those deceptively golden eyes.

It's not fair. I came to Muncie because I hoped it would finally be safe for me to settle down instead of going from human town to human town. Living among bloodsuckers wasn't my first choice, but I thought I could hide in plain sight. No shifter could enter the town without Roman knowing, so I should've been safe from my kind of supe at least.

And now I have to worry about vampires gunning for my blood?

It's still a better risk, I realize. I'd rather be bitten a hundred times over by a vampire than get mixed up with Jack Walker.

And I know that the Wicked Wolf will be coming for me eventually. If not me, then Gem, but she's up on Accalia with Ryker and her personal guard watching over her.

In Muncie, I've just got me.

Can vampires read minds? I have no idea, but when Roman frowns over at me, I'd bet anything I had that he knows exactly what I'm thinking about right at this moment.

Then he says, "And you have enemies of your own," and I'm sure of it.

Yup. He knows.

"I guess Dominic told you about last night." When he doesn't deny it, but just waits with an expectant expression, I try to explain. "I didn't invite her here. The shifter he saw me talking to. And you're right. I guess she is an enemy." Walker, too, but I keep that to myself. If Aleks wants to act like he doesn't know me, or where we could've possibly met before this, I'm not going to be the one to mention the shifter who forced him to participate in a fight to the death. "But I learned my lesson. She ambushed me when I left Muncie to visit Gemma Swann in Accalia. I won't do that again."

Out of the corner of my eyes, I watch for Aleks's reaction when I mention Gem. I don't know why I'm torturing myself, but it's like… I don't know. Like I have to see if he *will* react.

He does. I doubt I would've noticed if I wasn't looking for it, but his eyes flash brighter than the light fixtures hanging over our heads at just the mention of her name.

He doesn't say anything, though. He just keeps as quiet as ever as Roman continues addressing me.

"I understand. But, in Muncie, you'll still need someone to watch over you when I can't. You see, I rarely leave this building. I run the whole city from the Cadre's headquarters, and while my fang will keep you safe from most, there are still dangers, even here."

Now, I know that Gem was joking when she offered to give me one of her personal guard. With Roman's solemn tone, though, I'm beginning to second-guess my knee-jerk reaction to refuse even if she was kidding. Her guards—a trio of delta wolves, even though Jace was recently promoted to Pack Beta—were loyal to her and her alone, but maybe there was a packmate who wouldn't mind doing a little freelance guard duty for a Luna-touched female.

I open my mouth, prepared to ask Roman if he would open Muncie's border to a second shifter. It's the best idea I have other than packing up and going on the run again, but I barely get the first syllable out before I'm cut off.

"I will."

It's Aleks. No longer leaning against the wall, he's straight-backed and assured as he moves to stand opposite Roman's desk.

"Aleksander?"

"Me, Roman. I will guard Elizabeth."

What?

CHAPTER 7

Five months. I managed to avoid actually talking to my fated mate for five months.

Even after he showed up outside of my new home, watching me, leaving his scent behind... I could still pretend like I didn't know who he was. The teabags? For all I knew, it was a welcome gift automatically sent to anyone joining the Cadre. Gem made a point to tell me that he was as almost high up as Roman himself.

Now?

Now I can't.

"You don't have to do that."

"Yes, I do." His features are soft, pretty, but his jaw is so sharp, I bet I could cut a sheet of paper with it. "A threat to one of us is a threat to all. We can't put the city at risk."

Of course. Of freaking course that's the only reason he's volunteering. Not because of me. Not because he senses the same thing that the Luna insists: that we're fated mates. No. He's only agreeing to watch my back because of his duty to Muncie.

I pat the necklace. Addressing Roman, I ask, "Will this keep me safe while I'm within the borders?"

"From most, yes."

"And the patrol will keep any other shifters out?"

Aleks answers this time, brow slightly creased as if he knows where I'm going with this—and he doesn't like it. "They will."

"So then I don't need anyone watching over me. I appreciate the gesture," I say to Roman, "but I'm a she-wolf." And I'm so very tired of running. I've put roots down here, and I'm going to stay until I can't anymore. "To treat me as any less is kind of insulting."

"Roman, give me leave. Give me permission. Tell her that I'll be her guard."

"Aleksander." It's a warning tone I haven't heard from Roman yet. "Perhaps we should have this conversation after Elizabeth goes back to the lobby."

Aleks shakes his head so emphatically, his curls nearly bounce. "Not while she's in danger. Someone must keep her safe. It has to be me."

"Why?"

I want to echo Roman's simply stated question.

Why?

As if he heard my thoughts this time, Aleks turns to me. Just like me, he'd been avoiding looking straight at me we've been up here, but no longer. He peers directly into my eyes, pinning me into place with his gaze.

"Why? Because you're my beloved."

I blink, momentarily stunned. It breaks the stare, but even when my eyes shutter closed, the insistent expression on his face seems seared on the back of my eyelids.

I've known exactly who Aleksander Filan was to me all along, even when I was pretending I didn't. From the moment our eyes met when he was thrown in the pit and I was still at the Alpha's heel, the Luna told me that he was mine. I'd had dreams of a gorgeous male with pale green eyes before I ever saw him. When I did, it was like my dreams brought to life—only impossibly more beautiful.

However, the tug I felt toward him was so powerful, I could never be sure that he felt anything in return. It was one of the only times my "gift" failed *me*. Eventually, I convinced myself that he didn't. I had my reasons for staying away, but I've never heard of an able-bodied supe male purposely avoiding their fated mates—and for a vampire, their "beloved" counts—unless they were rejecting the bond.

What's worse? My fated mate not recognizing me

as his, or rejecting me instead? I clung to the first option because the second was soul-crushing.

And now, after five months, he's finally admitting what I would've never known for sure?

He's my fated mate—and I'm *his*?

Roman rises up from behind his desk. Switching from English to Russian, he says in an ominous tone, "Ona ne Julia, moy brat."

Julia again. Who is Julia?

I don't know, but Aleks surely does.

His eyes turn blood-red. "I know she's not Julia, Roman. Julia's been dead for two centuries."

She has? Two centuries... Gem said Aleks was more than two centuries old himself. Who is she—more importantly, who is the mysterious Julia to Aleks?

"You can't bring her back," Roman says, his voice softer than before. More soothing.

Aleks jerks his head, a rough nod. "I know that as well. But Elizabeth is here now, and she's in trouble. She might be wearing your fang, but we both know that's not enough. I will watch over her as well."

"Oh? You will?"

"No," I say, answering Roman before Aleks can. "He won't." Ignoring the determined look Aleks is shooting my way, I face the Cadre leader. "Is it okay if I go back downstairs now? I'm only scheduled until six and I want to finish some of the training work Leigh gave me."

"Elizabeth—"

"Of course," Roman says, speaking over Aleks. "Go on."

"*Roman.*"

"Stay behind with me, Aleksander. We have more to discuss."

Disappointment mingled with fury seethes off of Aleks. But, like the rest of the vampires in Muncie that I've met so far, he obeys Roman the same way that a pack does its Alpha.

I just hope Roman keeps him occupied until after my shift's over.

When I first feel the sudden chill creeping in, goosebumps popping up along my arms, I think it's because it's snowing again. Big, fat, white flakes are falling heavily from the night's sky. We're looking at another few inches by morning, and as much as I'm sick of the stuff, I can't deny that it doesn't look pretty as it coats the sidewalk, the grass, and the roads.

In fact, I drift over to the front window to get a better look—and that's when I realize that it might be cold out, but that wasn't what I was reacting to.

Aleks is standing outside of the townhouse again.

He hasn't been there long. In fact, judging by the

prints left in the snow, he must have just arrived when I got up to take a peek.

There's no time to duck and pretend I didn't see him. The second I moved the curtain, his head turned to see me silhouetted against the light. In one hand, he's holding a brown paper bag. He lifts the other, a friendly wave.

Unsure what else to do, I wave back.

As if that's all the permission he needs, Aleks bows his head, walking into the snow, striding purposely up my walkway.

I back away from the window, biting the claw on my right thumb.

The doorbell sounds.

I can't ignore it, can I?

Glancing down, I check to make sure I'm presentable. I've only been home for about an hour and a half. I kicked off my shoes as soon as I got in, but I'm still wearing my work clothes. My hair is piled high on top of my head in a messy bun. I wiped the make-up off of my face a couple of minutes ago, and had plopped down to watch some mindless tv before dinner in order to forget all about today's events.

You're my beloved...

You know what? Fine. Let's see if he likes at-home Elizabeth because if I'm his fated mate, so is she.

Almost as if I'm daring him to change his mind about his unexpected declaration, I shuffle over to the front door. Then, after taking a steadying breath so I don't look as nervous as I suddenly feel, I pull the door in.

"Aleks... um. Hi. What are you doing here?"

He holds up the bag. "My patrol starts at ten. I had some time so I thought I'd bring you dinner."

Oof. Good thing I'm leaning against the side of the door because the earnest way he says that? I need the support. I'd left him fuming in Roman's office, and his response is to bring me dinner?

"You didn't have to do that."

"Maybe before you knew that you were my beloved. But you know now, Elizabeth. And if I want to prove to you that you should accept me as your mate, this is one way to do it. A good mate provides, yes?"

"Uh. I guess."

"So you'll take it?"

Can I really say no?

I've never willingly accepted food from a male before. To do so while living in a pack has repercussions. But Aleks isn't trying to feed me the way a shifter male would. He's just trying to convince me that he meant what he said in Roman's office today.

Honestly, I don't know *what* to say.

A part of me wants to tell Aleks that he's meant to be mine. That the Luna has been telling me for more than five months now that he's my fated mate. But I can't. He's made a big leap, claiming me as his beloved.

If I tell him that my wolf recognizes him the same way he recognizes me… it'll be settled. I'll be a vampire's mate.

And I'm not ready for that.

But I can't say no, so I nod. "Yeah. Why not?"

"Where do you eat?"

This is so bizarre. And yet…

"Usually on a tray table in front of the television."

"In the living room?"

I nod.

"Tak. I've been here before. I know the way."

And, just like that, Aleks marches into the townhouse. He knocks the snow from his shoes, shaking the flakes from his water-dark curls, and comes inside without so much an invitation.

Guess pop culture got *that* wrong.

I chase after him, unsure what I'm supposed to do now. When I opened the door, I hadn't expected him to actually come inside, and now I have a vampire in my private space.

Even worse? My wolf is pleased to share it with her mate.

Aleks pulls the tray table away from the couch, gesturing for me to sit down. A little bit dazed at how quickly I lost control of this situation, I do. He places the tray table in front of me again, placing his brown paper bag on top of it.

Reaching in, he takes out a plastic container of

some kind of soup. It's white with hunks of sausage and egg floating in it. He pops the lid, then sets it in front of me. The spoon comes next. He places that next to the container.

"It should still be warm. If not, tell me, and I'll fix that for you."

I'm not getting out of eating this right now, am I?

He waits on bated breath as I scoop up some of the stew, then lift the spoon to my lips. When I swallow, he shudders out an exhale. "How does it taste?"

Sour and tangy, yet delicious. "It's good. What is it?"

"Bialy barszcz. In English, white borscht." He gives me a crooked grin that makes him that much more stunning—and a little more relatable. "I made it myself."

If he was a shifter, this would be courting behavior. Good thing he's not.

"Go on. Eat. It's hearty for this type of weather. Tea, too. I could make some if you'd like." He pauses for a moment before oh so causally asking, "Did you get my package?"

I was wondering if he was going to bring up the box he sent me. At least, now, I know why he felt compelled to send it.

"I did, thank you. I appreciated it. The soup, too. That was very... thoughtful of you."

"Consider it making amends for today. I could've broached the topic of your being my beloved a little more tactfully. I wasn't avoiding you, Elizabeth," he says, and once again I wonder about his mind-reading skills. "I was hoping to ease you into knowing who we are to each other but I no longer have the luxury for that."

I hurriedly spoon a chunk of sausage into my mouth, taking my time to chew it. Sorry, Aleks. Can't talk. Mouth full.

He smiles again, before moving so that he's standing next to the far side of my couch. Hiking up his trousers, he sits down. Not once does he take his eyes off of me, almost as if he's getting pleasure out of watching me eat his food.

He should. It's pretty yummy.

As I make quick work of the meal, his gaze finally begins to wander over the room. I know he said he's been here before—when Gem lived at the townhouse, I'm sure—so he seems interested in how I've made it my own space. Too bad there isn't much to see. I came here with very little, and most of the changes I did make were upstairs in my bedroom.

Not that Aleks is going to see that anytime soon.

When he notices the wooden box that I have sitting on the side table next to the couch, he asks, "Are those your cards?"

"My cards?"

"Your fortune-telling cards. I've seen you with them before."

How? I never used them in Muncie. They're specifically for when I'm fleecing human tourists. So how the hell does Aleks know about them?

With an openly suspicious glance at him, I nod slowly. "My tarot cards. Yes."

"Would you read me?"

Huh?

"Me? I mean, I'm not an actual fortune-teller. I just faked it for the humans to get money, that's all."

"Entertainment, then?"

"I guess you could say so."

"Okay." Aleks settles deeper into the couch. He props one ankle over his knees, his arms stretched along the back. "I wouldn't mind being entertained."

Yup. Totally out of control.

I have to make this work for me. But how?

Ah. I think I have an idea...

"Let's make a deal. When I do a reading for a client, I pull three cards. I'll do the same for you, but I want you to answer three questions for me first. What do you think?"

His eyes glimmer with open interest. "I think you have a deal. I'm through hiding. To you, I'll be an open book. Ask me anything."

My first question is easy. I don't even have to think about it before I'm asking, "Am I really yours?"

I've known for five months that Aleks was my fated mate. Longer, really. For years, I dreamed of a gorgeous male with his carelessly tousled curls and a pair of seafoam green eyes that I could drown in. He was so otherworldly beautiful, I knew he could only be a product of my lonely imagination. He couldn't be real.

But he was.

When I saw him being forced into the pit, I could barely believe it. I *knew* him even before I ever learned his name.

My question is easy. So, it seems, is his answer.

"Yes."

Because I don't want to give anything away with my expression, I busy myself with opening the wooden box I keep my tarot cards in. Lifting them out, I give the deck a cursory shuffle.

It takes a couple of seconds before I have my next question.

"Do vampires form bonds like shifters do?"

"They can, and they do. Like your kind, we can choose our beloved, but Fate also has her say. You see, blood tells."

"What does that mean?"

"I don't have a beast inside of me or," he adds with a pointed nod at me, "a goddess guiding me, but a vampire has a second sense about these things. We can look at a prospective mate and know that they're meant for us and us alone. With a single taste, though, it's undeniable. And it would only strengthen any existing tie the more we drink. By the way, that should be your second question, but I'm enjoying this game. You still have two more."

I ignore his slight tease as I focus on the way he said *we*. As he spoke, I noticed that his fangs grew longer. Sharper. Almost as if he's getting ready to do just that. Suddenly, I realize that we're not just talking about the differences between our kinds of supes anymore.

I keep a wary eye on the points of his fangs as I ask, "Do you want to bite me?"

From the sudden hunger in his gaze, I can tell that he's dying to. "Yes."

"Oh."

"Don't be afraid of me, Elizabeth. I won't unless you invite me to."

So it's like being invited into my bedroom then? *Never.*

And yet—

"Would it hurt? Being bitten, I mean."

"Vampires can give pleasure or pain with their bite. As my beloved, I would never see you in pain. So no." He gestures at the cards with his chin. "And that's your three. Now it's my turn."

With a shrug, I pull three cards for him.

Oh, come *on*.

"Like I said, I'm really just a fraud. When I read the cards, they don't mean anything."

Gathering up the cards together, I stack them on

the bottom of the deck, eager to change the subject. Even though that's true, it's too much of a coincidence that the three cards I pulled for Aleks are actually pretty fitting: The Moon, the Lovers, and Death. I couldn't have picked a better set of three if I cheated.

Aleks leans forward. He shifts, lowering both of his shoes to the floor as he turns to me. "Are you sure about that?"

I drop the cards back into the box. "Can I ask you one more question?"

"You can."

"Who is Julia?"

Aleks sits up from his slouch. The companionable air that had settled around us as we played the question game disappears immediately.

"No one you need to worry about."

He's lying, murmurs the Luna. *In this, he hides from you.*

Roman never explained who she was. When I mentioned her name to Gem during our dinner the other day, she said that Julia was a female that Aleks once loved before hurriedly adding that it wasn't her story to tell. I'd have to ask Aleks if I wanted to know more.

And Aleks, I'm absolutely convinced now, never will.

Of course not.

What am I doing? Why am I playing this game

with him? He says he's an open book, but at the first sign that I've asked him a question he doesn't want to answer, he shuts down.

And maybe I did the same thing when it comes to the cards.

Still.

I never thought I'd have a mate of my own. Living in fear that a single touch would break any bond I made with another, I long ago gave up on the hope that there might be someone who loved me so irrevocably that they never doubted that we belonged together forever.

And Aleks won't be able to do that, either. I'm sure of it.

Getting up, ignoring my wolf's keening whine, I cross the living room. Grabbing the doorknob, I give it such a hard turn, I nearly snap it off.

"You should be getting ready for your patrol."

"I still have another hour."

He's really going to make me kick him out, isn't he?

"I'm tired. I think you should go."

"But—"

"Good night, Aleksander."

"Elizabeth, your *eyes*..."

That's right. You're not the only one who can change their eye color when you're experiencing strong emotions. Only I'm not feeling bloodlust like he does when his eyes go from green to red.

For me, my eyes change from silver to black when I can't control myself.

And, as I've just discovered, when it comes to Aleks, I don't think I'll ever be able to.

An hour later, I'm still struggling to come to terms with what a difference a day can make. Yesterday, I was sure he had no idea who I was. Early this evening, I learned he thought of me as his beloved. And now? Now I'm sure that he's set into motion his pursuit of me—right when I've accepted that I can never have him.

That's not all, either. Aleks never mentioned how the rest of his discussion with Roman went, but considering he felt comfortable enough to bring me dinner? I'm thinking that he convinced my boss to give him the okay to watch over me.

Well… if that's the case? I might as well give him something to watch.

I need to get out of the townhouse. I need to run. Because I'm so close to both my wolf and the Luna, I don't have to shift as often as more powerful wolves do, but if I go too long in my skin, I get antsy. After the meeting with Roman and Aleks? I have this urge to run until my pads are bloody and my wolf collapses on her belly.

As soon as I'm sure Aleks has left, I trade my outfit for a simple shift dress. My shoes are slip-ons, and I go without a purse. At this hour, I don't have any intention to go anywhere but the only patch of dense forest and greenery in all of Muncie; even in winter, the evergreens provide cover. It's the closest to wild land as I can get while living in an urban city, and it's the sole place I feel free to let my wolf loose.

It's one of Roman's rules. If I want to stay in Muncie, I needed to keep any unsuspecting humans from finding out that shifters—and, by extension, *vampires*—exist. That means no shifting in front of anyone else, no walking around on the streets while I was still in my fur, and no running unless I'm concealed in the trees.

I'm probably pushing my luck. My wolf will leave actual prints that won't be too easy to explain, but right now? I don't care. If Roman is pissed, I'll deal with it later.

I just need to *run*.

Once I'm about thirty feet past the border of the trees, I take a deep breath. It smells like snow and frozen earth and that's about all. No one else is within scenting distance. Quickly shucking my dress, I fold it neatly. I tuck my discarded shoes beneath it.

When all I'm wearing is a sliver of the moon and Roman's fang, I reach inside of myself, giving control over to my wolf. Where dark-haired, silver-eyed Elizabeth was standing seconds ago, there's now an arctic white wolf with similar eyes that glimmer beneath the moonlight.

I wasn't sure if the chain would transform with me. Jewelry has a tendency to—like rings and earrings—while clothes don't. Shaking my wolfish head, I can see that the chain is gone, but it's not broken on the crusted snow beneath my paws. It's still on the two-legged form waiting inside for the run to be over.

The quaint breeze ruffles my fur. My ears twitch when it whispers through the branches on some of the empty trees. Rearing back, I pounce, chuffing when my paws land in a pile of powder and it puffs up, tickling my snout.

When I'm presenting as a human, everything is made up of shades of grey. As a wolf? Things are black and white. Aleks is my mate. The wintry weather is fun. The park has some tiny prey I can chase.

My wolf wants to run.

So I do.

CHAPTER 8

I run for a couple of hours, reveling in the sensation of being in my fur. I make laps, careful to stay inside the wooded land. At one point, I think I hear someone approaching, but instead of playing a stalking game with them, I head downwind, then put some distance between us.

Before long, though, my stomach starts to growl. In the winter, most prey is hibernating. The mice I chased would be nothing but a mouthful for my wolf and I didn't bother. After expending so much energy, I needed more than that, and Aleks's borscht is a distant memory by now.

Making my way through the words, I pad back toward where I left my pile of clothes. Resting on my haunches, I shift, then push myself off of the ground before bending over and grabbing my dress.

I'm just yanking it over my head when I sense that I'm not alone anymore.

Fresh out of a shift, my senses are a little hazy. Everything is much keener when I'm a wolf which means that my nose seems duller, my vision less acute. After a couple of minutes, I'll adjust, but when the vampiric scent and powerful aura brushes up against my back, I'm not so sure I *have* a few minutes before I have to face him.

Still, I call his name as I slip my bare feet into my shoes. "Aleksander—"

Not yours, murmurs the Luna.

What?

Of course it's Aleks. What other vampire would have tracked me down to the edge of the woods?

I don't know why I thought I knew better than the Luna. Spinning around, the skirt of my dress flaring around me, I expect to find Aleks watching me, just like he told Roman he would.

But my goddess, as ever, was right. It's not Aleks.

At least I understand why the aura seemed as powerful as his. It's because I'm not looking at one vampire.

There are *two* standing a few feet away, watching me with intent expressions.

The one on the right is about a head shorter than his companion. He has black hair that falls to his chin, pale blue eyes, and a pointed nose. The vampire on the left is taller. Bald. I don't know what his eyes normally look like but, as he runs his gaze over me, they're already the tell-tale red of bloodlust.

He's also sneering at me in a way that has my claws unsheathing.

Roman's fang is tucked beneath my dress. I want to show it to them, to let them know that they shouldn't be looking at me like that—like I'm prey—but I stop when I realize that my claws are out. That's a sure sign that I'm a wolf shifter, something I'm suddenly eager to conceal.

I will them back. With my wolf so freshly in control, it's hard to banish them, but I try.

I need to show them the fang. Before I get the chance, though, the shorter of the two nudges the other vampire in the side.

"What do you think, Hector. Is that her?"

Hector—the bald, sneering vampire—gives me a look of disgust. "Don't you scent Zakharov on her? Of course it is."

"She's a shifter? She doesn't seem like one of the dogs." His nostrils flare. "Doesn't smell like one, either. You're right. I only get Zakharov."

I smell like Roman? Must be because of the fang I'm wearing.

But if they know that Roman offered me his protection, why aren't they backing off?

Unless... unless they're some of the vampires that Roman warned me about earlier tonight.

Uh oh.

"Don't you remember, Anton?" Hector says, his low voice a rumble. "That's what the other one said. What makes this one so dangerous. You don't know that she's a shifter until it's too late."

Anton's curious look turns cautious. "Hurry. Let's do what we came here for."

I brace myself. If these two come any closer, I'm either going to use my claws against them or, if I can shift fast enough, my wolf's fangs. I have no clue what they came after me for, but I'm not going to let them get away with it.

And then Hector strokes his clean-shaven chin, his eyes still blood-red. "I have a better idea."

"We're supposed to bring her to the border, make the trade. Those are the orders. That's why we're here."

"I know. But that was before I realized what this means. Sure, we could give a dog to another. Or... and hear me out... this is Zakharov's new female. It will weaken him to throw her back to the wolves. But if we kill her, leaving her drained body outside of his precious headquarters..."

Anton's blue eyes light up. "It'll destroy him."

"Exactly."

Oh my Luna. For a second, I was so stuck when they mentioned something about dogs—a vampire's derogatory name for wolf shifters—that I didn't really understand the rest of what Hector said. When I do, though?

I'm *stunned*.

They're... they're talking about draining me. Killing me. Leaving me for Roman to find. And I'm the fucking idiot who's still standing here, listening to these two bloodsuckers plot my fate without doing anything to stop them. I could be attacking. I could be running away. I could be doing anything—but I'm not.

What the hell is wrong with me?

My eyes turn black. Neither one of these vampires have a bond with another, or even the promise of one. I can't use that against them, but do they know that?

"Back off," I tell them, my voice vibrating with the power I've drawn from the Luna herself. It's more effective against another shifter—it isn't often that I use the Luna against them, but I have the ability to control them if I choose to—but even vampires can sense that I'm not just another supe when I get like this. "Leave me or else I'll—"

"Elizabeth."

Yours, says the Luna, my borrowed power returning to her as quickly as it came.

Aleks.

I nearly sag with relief. Nearly, since my instincts warn against giving these two vampires something to use against me. If they know that I have any kind of tie to Aleks, this could get uglier than it's about to.

"Evening, Aleksander."

If he notices the cold way I'm addressing him, he doesn't act like it. Then again, considering how we left things back in Roman's office—not to mention me kicking him out of the townhouse—he probably is expecting a less than happy welcome from me.

"Are you done with your run?"

Even as I nod, I can't help but think: Huh. So he *was* watching. At least long enough to know what I spent the last few hours doing.

Did he watch me shift? See me naked?

Do I *want* him to have seen me naked?

What took him so long to realize I was in trouble—

"Enough!"

While Anton had taken a few steps' retreat when Aleks strode over to where we were, Hector refused to back down. Now, looking even bigger than before, his fangs lengthening past his bottom lip, he turns a murderous gaze on Aleks.

"Filan. Leave us. This has nothing to do with you."

"Oh?" He sounds pleasant, but the hard look in his eyes tells us all that he's anything but. If I didn't believe to the depths of my soul that, despite not knowing him at all, he'd never hurt me... I would've bolted at that single syllable. "It doesn't?"

"No."

Aleks *tsks*. "That's where you're wrong, Hector. This has everything to do with me."

"You've been loyal to Zakharov for too long."

"Maybe. But your rebellion… it won't work. Monroe has already lost his head. So has Stefan. You all seek out death, so eager to join Marcel. When will you learn that Roman *is* the Cadre?"

"Roman is a male like the rest of us. See if he can stay so heartless and cold when we present his drained female to him."

Up until then, Aleks kept the conversation loose. Casual.

Not anymore.

"She's not his," he retorts with enough emotion that I suck in a breath.

The shorter vampire—Anton—glances from Aleks to me. He must be smarter than his pal because understanding flares in his blood-red eyes.

"She wears his fang—"

"She's not Roman's, Hector. She's *mine*."

My heart leaps into my throat.

The bald vampire's face twists in an expression so fierce, I fight the urge to cling to Aleks's back. Meanwhile, Anton must really know which way the wind is blowing because, while his buddy's attention is on Aleks, he disappears into the trees.

"Two blows with one kill," Hector says, bounding on the balls of his feet, preparing to launch himself at me. "A message to Roman and his most devoted servant then."

In the blink of an eye, Aleks moves from five feet away from us to directly in front of me. "You have to get through me first."

"*Gladly.*"

"Stay back, Elizabeth," he commands right before he intercepts Hector.

He doesn't have to tell me twice. I scurry backward, looking for cover, as the two males collide.

Vampires don't feed off of each other. When Hector bares his fangs, he has every intention of going for Aleks's throat if only to tear it out. At the same time, Aleks hammers him with blows, pushing him away from me, while jabbing his fangs in every part of Hector's flesh he can find.

I watched Aleks fight once before this. It was a massacre. I didn't know if all vampires had the same skill, but now that I'm watching the two of them, I notice that Aleks is a much more effective killer.

Hector figures that out about the same time that I do. Realizing that he won't win a clean fight, he reaches behind him, pulling a weapon out from somewhere.

The moon reflects against the blade. I know immediately that it's made of silver, a metal known to weaken supes.

In a shifter challenge, no one uses weapons. Our claws and our fangs and our beasts are all we need. It's just not done. Even Christian only wielded a gun after a challenge, never before.

I can't let him use it.

Cupping my hands around my mouth, I shout out, "Knife!"

Later, I still won't be sure if I made a mistake. Because Aleks? When he hears my voice, he immediately glances over at me. That split second of him focusing on me instead of the fight is all Hector needs. He buries the knife in Aleks's side.

I scream.

Aleks *roars*.

With the knife buried to the hilt inside of him, Aleks whips his head around. He shoots out both of his hands, reaching for Hector's neck. You would never know the silver affected him since, with impressive strength, he tugs Hector by the throat up to his fangs, biting a huge chunk out of the vampire. Hector gurgles on his own blood, flailing, while Aleks tightens his grip on Hector's neck.

The next thing I know, his head is in Aleks's grip, his body crumpling to the frozen earth. Aleks punts it with his expensive dress shoe before rolling Hector's head like it's a freaking bowling ball.

As I gape at him, he drops to his knees. With a grunt, he yanks the knife out of his side, flinging it far, far away from him.

I rush over to him. He's covered in blood, his eyes

in full bloodlust mode, his fangs extended longer than I've ever seen on any vampire. But when I throw myself to the dirt in front of him, he lifts a shaky hand, wiping his face with the back of the other as if trying to make himself more presentable.

I could give a shit. "Aleks? Aleks! Are you okay?"

"Yes." He closes his eyes, taking a few seconds to gain some control. When he opens them again, they're light green rimmed with red. "I wish you hadn't seen that."

I'm not. Shifters respect strength; Aleks is strong. They understand being challenged and having to fight to the death. Aleks did both multiple times now.

I just... I wish I hadn't distracted him long enough for Hector to attempt to gut him with that knife this time.

"I'm fine," I tell him honestly. Some of the blood spray stained my dress, but apart from that? I'm perfectly fine. "But you... he got you with the knife. I know you'll heal eventually, but how bad is it?"

Aleks immediately clamps his hand over the bloody wound in his side. "Not bad at all."

Good to know. Aleks is a shit liar, too.

"Please. Let me see."

He hesitates, but eventually lowers his hand again.

"Oh." I gulp. "Yeah. That's bad."

Bad? He's probably lost more blood than a vampire can afford to, and it's still oozing out.

"Nothing that a few feedings won't cure, księżyca. Don't fret for me."

Kher-zhitza.

Okay, then.

I have no idea what that means, but if he wants to call me that, that's fine. I mean, if it wasn't for Aleks, Hector would've gone for my throat. I'm nowhere near as strong as Aleks. I wouldn't have survived. He can call me whatever the hell he wants.

I owe him my life.

Repay him. Feed your mate.

Give him your blood.

When I recoil at the Luna's suggestion, Aleks glances away. "I should be going. I must inform Roman about this."

Aleks is already pale, but beneath the moonlight, he's lost any of the color he already had. And he wants to go make a report to his boss?

Maybe the Luna *is* right. I think… I think he needs to feed.

I gulp, then scoot closer to him. "Wait. Aleks… before you go, have some of my blood."

He goes motionless.

I nod. Hours ago, I swore I'd never let him bite me. How quick things change… "I've got plenty, and you need some. Take mine."

His gaze slides over to me, searching my face. "Are you sure?"

"You wouldn't have gotten hurt if it wasn't for me," I point out. "It's the least I can do. And you told me it wouldn't hurt."

He wants to do it. I don't know how I know for sure, but Aleks wants a taste of my blood more than he wants anything else at this moment.

Still, he resists. "I can find another donor. It doesn't have to be you."

"You fed me tonight," I remind him. "Let me return the favor."

Aleks frowns. "For reasons I'm sure you understand, I fed you, yes. I didn't do it because I expected you to reciprocate."

Right. Because I'm supposed to be his beloved.

And he's supposed to be my mate.

"Will you heal faster if you have some now?" When he doesn't answer, I can't keep myself from prodding. "Will you? You can't protect Muncie if you're half-drained."

He can't protect you, the Luna adds. *Remind him.*

Following my goddess's lead, I echo, "You can't protect me."

That does it. Slowly climbing to his feet, Aleks stumbles, then straightens. Once he's steady, he offers me his hand, helping me up until I'm positioned directly in front of him.

Hoping that I'm doing this right, I tilt my head, baring my throat to him.

He moves into me. His hands land on my shoulders, his eyes completely red again as he forces back a shudder.

"Will it... will it hurt?" I whisper. He already told me it wouldn't, but I'm a coward. Those fangs of his look even sharper this close. I have to make sure.

With the points of his fangs mere millimeters from my neck, the chill of Aleks's breath cools my overheated skin as he vows, "I'll never hurt you, księżyca."

And then, before I can ask him what he keeps calling me, Aleks plunges them into my skin.

He's true to his word. After a slight pinch, I feel nothing except the strange sensation of something pulling on my neck. It's vaguely uncomfortable at first, and I find myself hoping that he'll be done soon, when, out of nowhere, heat starts pooling low in my belly.

It... it feels *good*.

As he sucks, I melt against him. The pleasure rises, and after a few more seconds, I moan.

He groans in answer, increasing the pace of his suction.

All too soon, though, he stops. Releasing his fangs with a gentle *pop*, I'm panting as I realize that I started grinding my pussy against him. My skirt rode up slightly, though not enough that Aleks is able to see that I'm panty-free right now.

My vampire? He's hard as a rock, his erection a

thick bulge that I was rubbing against while he was biting me.

I shouldn't be embarrassed, but I am. He's my fated mate, and I'm dry-humping him after offering my blood to heal his wound. What the hell is wrong with me?

I start to back away from him—but he doesn't let me.

His eyes a rich blazing red, fangs impossibly longer, he grips my shoulders, holding me steady.

In a flash, I suddenly remember what he said before. How he would know for sure if I was truly his beloved—his vampire mate—as soon as he tasted my blood.

And I just served myself up on a silver platter for him.

From the way he's holding onto me so tightly, he's about to head back for seconds. As he crouches slightly, putting us on the same level that his dick is only separated from my pussy by a few layers of clothes on his part, I wonder if we're about to go one step further as mates.

Will I let him?

Better question: can he stop me from initiating?

But he doesn't do either of those things, and I don't know what to think. No biting. No fucking. Instead—with his fangs still fully extended, and his eyes an unholy red—he goes to *kiss* me.

With his mouth full of my blood, and his erection grinding against me, Aleks wants to kiss me for the first time.

I can deal with the blood. I've tasted far worse. But with the Luna's voice in my head and my wolf keening for her mate, I know it won't stop there. Not tonight. Two seconds ago, I wondered if he was about to unzip his pants, throw up my skirt, and shove himself inside of me. I would've let him, too. If I don't get away from him now, I still would.

So a kiss?

I *can't*.

Aleks leans into me. I turn my head just as his lips brush my cheek. They're warm, I notice; his breath, too. Drinking from me has turned him from the undead to a warm-blooded male.

When I avoid his kiss, Aleks immediately reacts like one. You would've thought I slapped him across the face instead of simply turning away.

Aleks lets go, shoving himself away from me before coming back, like we're two magnets that can't help but be pulled together.

He reaches for me, fisting his hands before we touch as he says in a rasp of a voice, "You deny me. You deny *us*?"

His chest is heaving, his cheeks hollowed as he breathes in deep.

That should've been my first warning. Vampires are

one of the undead. None of their kind needs to breathe. But he's heaving, and like before, I'm the idiot who forgets when she's supposed to get the hell away from a threat.

Then again, my mate is never supposed to be a threat...

His hand lashes out. Crooked fingers grab my chain. A brutal twist has the links breaking in two as Aleks snatches Roman's fang from me.

"You're mine, Julia—"

Julia?

Julia.

Again!

My wolf lets out a pained yip, like she's been kicked in the side. I gasp, swallowing the sound before my two-legged form can utter it.

Aleks pulls back, horrified. Even if I wanted to pretend that he hadn't just said that, his reaction makes it impossible. I don't even know if he's more upset by his slip-up or the way he just ripped Roman's fang from my neck, but it doesn't matter.

I have had *enough*.

"Julia might be," I snap at him, clamping my hand over the marks he left on my neck. They'll be gone by morning—I'll make sure of that—but I already regret my reckless offer since the vampire *doesn't even know my name*. "But I'm not her, whoever she is. My name is *Elizabeth*."

I kick off my shoes. My dress? It's tatters as I fall back, letting my wolf take over again, shifting shapes in the blink of an eye.

Aleks shouts after me, but it sounds like so much noise as I tear off through the woods. Right then, I could care less that I'm breaking all of Roman's rules. After the way *three* of his vampires have treated me tonight, I think I should get a pass.

Especially since Aleks immediately starts chasing after me.

Good luck.

He might be fast, but nothing can catch up to a wounded shifter trying to outrun rejection.

Once again, turns out that I'm wrong.

Julia...

I guess he can't call me whatever he wants after all.

CHAPTER 9

I didn't realize how much I'd grown to rely on Roman's fang—and his protection—until I don't have it anymore.

Luckily, my ability to shield my scent whenever I want to gives me a little wiggle room to work with. Any vampire I met would be able to tell that I'm some kind of supe, but as long as I'm in my skin, they can't be sure that I'm a shifter. No reason to ask Roman for another one.

He'll know. Of course he will. But I'm not going to be the one who brings it to his attention. If he wants to know where the fang went, he can ask Aleks. Last I know, he had it clenched tightly in his fist, leaving me to run the rest of the way to my townhouse without it.

It was probably for the best. Roman was right. The fang had put an even bigger target on my back. Those two vampires came after me for a reason, but the lead one—Hector, the one Aleks killed—had changed his mind when he realized that I had Roman's fang on.

Let Aleks deal with that. At least he's proven that he can destroy his fellow vampires as easily as taking down a shifter.

He was ruthless, yet beautiful, showing no mercy as he savagely ripped Hector's throat open with his fangs. When he fought Jasper, the shifter back in the district, he'd been just as fierce. Beneath his pretty face and his noble nature, he's a cold-hearted killer.

And there's no way that should turn me on as much as it does.

Hey. I'm a shifter. Being attracted to strength—knowing that he would be a provider *and* a protector—is kind of part of the deal.

Then there's just how good it felt to have his fangs in my neck, warm lips sucking intently, pulling the blood from my veins as I was able to provide something for him.

Until he, you know, called me by another female's name.

I had hoped he might give me some time to lick my wounds. I should've known better. A supe is a supe, after all, and males courting their mates just don't know when to stop.

Midway through my next shift, right before my lunch hour, he enters the lobby of the Cadre building.

He tries to catch my eye, but I was prepared. One good thing about him being a powerful vamp? His aura is unmistakable, and so is his scent. Now that I know to look for it, I can catch his approach from a few blocks away so that, when he strides inside of the lobby, my nose is already buried in a mound of paperwork.

Sorry, Aleks. Too busy to say hi.

You understand.

Does that stop him? An overbearing vampire who has finally decided that I'm his?

Not even a little.

He has a plastic bag in his hand. "I brought you lunch. I noticed that you usually bring some from home, but when you don't, you prefer eating at the deli down the street. I got you a ham and turkey sandwich. Cheese, no lettuce."

My exact order.

Did I need the reminder that he's been my shadow for weeks? Nope. Will I read too much into the seemingly friendly gesture? Aleks is a supe, so hell fucking yes.

"Thank you."

"Will you eat it, księżyca?"

"We'll see. Like you said, I usually pack my own lunch. Maybe Leigh wants it."

Leigh is a vampire. She takes lunch, but it's never where I see her. So, yeah... I don't think she wants my sandwich.

He exhales, his aura going arctic.

Uh-oh. I think I touched a nerve.

There's something about Aleks. Maybe it's because he's my fated mate, I don't know. Because, while his dominance and power level are attractive to me, I don't feel the need to submit to him; at least, not the way I would the Alpha. He's strong, but I can stand on my own two feet around him without the fear of being bulldozed.

"Is there another reason why you're here? Can I help you with something?"

Leigh—who had been watching the exchange with an interested eye—cuts in. "He arranged for a meeting with Roman. He's waiting for you, Aleksander."

Aleks gives me one last searching look before nodding. "Let him know I'm on my way up."

"Of course." She makes the call as Aleks reluctantly heads toward the elevator. Once he's gone and she's hung up the phone again, she scoots her chair closer to me. "Okay, Elizabeth. Spill."

I should've expected this. Anyone who thinks that a shifter pack is full of gossips has obviously never met vampires.

"It's nothing." At her disbelieving look, I flush. "He's gotten the idea in his head that I'm his beloved."

Leigh's eyes widen. "Are you?"

Am I?

I shrug. "I don't know. It's... it's complicated."

"Trust me. I know all about complicated. When I first met Tamera, I thought I was straight. Had no idea I was bisexual until we met and I felt a pull toward her that I couldn't deny. But while 'complicated' is never easy, it can work out in the end. Look at us. We've been mated for sixty years and we're even looking for our third."

"Your *third*? What, like a third mate?"

She laughs. "Don't worry. I think you're pretty, but we already have our intended in mind."

My cheeks are immediately on fire. "No. I didn't think you were hitting on me. I just... shifters only get one fated mate. We can choose to take a different one if we want, but once the bond is made, it's for life." Or until my "gift" breaks it. "I guess I thought it was the same for vampires."

"Ah. I get it. Yeah, vampires are a little different than that. We share our blood to make our bonds. We can't feed off of each other... we can only get sustenance from shifters or humans... but the blood exchange builds bonds. You're right. Once we have one, we can't break it, but we can make as many as we want as long as it's consensual."

So that's why Aleks is convinced I'm his beloved? And why he courted Gem the same way? Because, as a vampire, he could've loved his Julia, somehow lost her, then moved on to try to develop a bond with another.

Oh. I... I don't know what to think about that.

Having been born and raised knowing that I'll only be lucky enough to have *one* mate, discovering that my fated mate could have many.

That's definitely something to think about—and I still am about a half an hour later when Aleks steps off of the elevator and approaches the lobby desk again.

I glance up from the papers in front of me when I sense his aura heading toward me. I'm looking to see if he's going to stride right through the lobby's door, but he doesn't.

He moves toward the desk, stopping right in front of me.

"Elizabeth?"

"Yes?"

"May I speak to you?"

I hesitate for a moment, struggling to come up with a plausible reason to refuse. When I can't, I nod. "I guess."

"If you're worried about your work, I already asked Roman for permission."

"Oh?" I try to keep my expression calm. Unaffected. Useless when I'm surrounded by other supes, but at least I *try*. "Was that before or after you apologized to him for yanking his fang off of my neck?"

His eyes flash. "I don't apologize," he says, "but I... I explained the situation to him. He understands."

I'm glad he does. "In that case, I think I should go back to work—"

"I don't apologize," he says again, "and I can count the times I have between two hands. But, for you, księżyca, I offer one. I'm sorry about last night."

If it's as rare as he claims, I should just accept it— but I can't. Not while I don't know what exactly he thinks he's apologizing for.

Was it taking Roman's fang and leaving me defenseless to the other supes in Muncie? Was it getting pissed when I decided not to kiss him? Or, I don't know, was it calling me another female's name?

"What part of it?"

"Excuse me?"

"What part are you sorry for?"

Aleks's gaze flickers past me. Out of the corner of my eye, I can see that Leigh is watching us with rapt attention, not even bothering to hide it.

Clearing his throat, he gestures with his head toward the entrance. "Perhaps we can have this discussion in private."

Of course. Why wouldn't he want to do that?

I follow Aleks as he guides me through the doors, leading me a few feet away from the entrance. When he turns to face me again, his gaze is immediately drawn to my neck.

"Don't get any ideas," I huff. "I'm off the menu."

He nods. "I understand. And I should probably apologize for that, too, but... I'd be lying if I said I was sorry that I tasted you. For a hint of your blood, Elizabeth, I'd risk your wrath and more."

The idea that he wants to bite me again should not be as sexy as it is. It takes everything I have not to offer my neck in submission. It feels right to do so, but I just manage to resist the urge.

"If you won't apologize about that," I say after a few moments of tension, "then what are you apologizing for?"

"For not explaining myself before now." Reaching into his pocket, Aleks pulls out a chain. I choke on a gasp, assuming it's the same sort of chain as the one Roman gave me, but it's not. Instead of a fang hanging off of it, it's a metal pendant.

No. A locket.

Using his thumbnail, Aleks flicks it open.

Inside the locket, there's a picture.

"Who is this?" I breathe out.

Because it isn't me. It looks like me, so much so that I can't believe what I'm seeing, but it's *not* me.

I know she's not Julia, Roman...

Don't let it be her. Don't let it be the female that everyone keeps mentioning—

"Julia Złoty."

Of course it is.

So many of our features match. Her wide forehead. The slope of her nose. Her plump mouth. The shape of her jaw. Even the color of her hair.

It's a portrait, an old-fashioned painting, but it could easily be a picture of me—except for her eyes. They're not silver. They're a bright, gleaming golden shade.

Vampires don't have eyes that color. Neither do humans.

"She was a wolf shifter?"

"Julia was an alpha." Aleks's nod is jerky and short as he snaps the locket shut. "She was also my beloved before her death two centuries ago."

I want to say that it's just like I thought, just like I guessed even thought I never spoke my suspicions out loud, but it's not.

It's so much worse.

His former beloved isn't just another shifter. She isn't even just a rare alpha, considered by my kind to be the Luna reborn like Gemma.

His Julia is my twin, and now I can't shake the feeling that I'm simply her replacement.

"Thank you for showing me that." I mean it, too. After what Leigh said, I'd started to think that maybe —*maybe*—there was a chance for us. Now that I've learned the truth about Julia? There's no fucking way. "If you'll excuse me, though, I really do have to go back to work."

I'm just reaching the door to the lobby when Aleks calls after me.

"You must know that Roman is only keeping you close because you're valuable to him."

I don't turn around. I just shoot back, "At least I'm valuable to someone," before leaving him out on the corner by himself.

As I take my seat, Leigh doesn't ask me what happened with Aleks. She just takes one look at my face, then announces, "You need a distraction."

"I need to work," I mumble. That's all the distraction I need.

"No. Really. Listen, me and Tamera are going to Mea Culpa after sundown tonight. Gretchen, too. It's a vamp club, but you're one of us now. Cadre. You should come with."

"I don't know…"

"Come on, Elizabeth. You said it yourself. Your situation with Aleksander is complicated. Why not have one night where it isn't?"

You know what? She has a point.

"Will they let me in?" This is Muncie. A Fang City. It's a pretty valid concern. "With me being a shifter, I mean."

Her eyes sparkle. "If you're with us? Trust me, girl. Not only will they let you in, you won't have to buy your own drinks all night."

Considering it's a vampire club, I probably won't partake, but it's the thought that counts.

"Okay. I'll go."

HINT OF HER BLOOD

Gem calls the three female vampires the Nightmare Trio. If she finds out that I've actually become *friends* with them, I'm sure I'll hear an earful from her. Just because Gretchen, Leigh, and Tamera thought they could feed off of her when she first drove out of Accalia and into Muncie, she's harbored a grudge.

And, okay. That's a pretty good reason. But they've always been nice to me. Even Gretchen, who, despite her comments, has never actually been that malicious to me whenever she stops by to flirt with Leigh.

I meet them about a block out of Mea Culpa, anxiously tugging on the hem of my dress. It took a couple of blocks before I grew used to the wobble of my high heels, and I'm glad tonight isn't as windy as it has been. For the first time in ages, I took care with my hair and my make-up, and I would've hated for the wintry weather to ruin it.

They're already waiting for me, each one more of a knock-out than the last. I made a good choice, getting as dressed up as I did, because the three of them are so inhumanly stunning that they look like they belong in a photoshopped ad straight out of a high-class magazine.

Not only that, but their cheeks are flushed. Clearly,

the three gorgeous vampires have already had their dinner.

As I walk over to them, I'm treated to a once-over by each of them. Holding my breath, I wait to see if they think I look good enough to join them inside of the club.

After how much I spent on this slinky dress, I hope so.

Roman, I've learned, is a very generous boss. When he hired me, he made it clear that he was keeping me close because of my ability. Sticking me in the lobby with Leigh had been a good way to explain what I was doing there, and I'm becoming a pretty decent receptionist. Make no mistake, though. When he had an envelope full of cash waiting for me this morning as payment for my first week, it wasn't my typing skills or my phone-answering that had him giving me as much as he had.

Am I complaining? Not even a little. I'll break as many bonds as he wants me to—so long as the bonded mates *want* to be separated from each other like Dominic and Felicity did.

Look at me. Elizabeth Howell, vampire divorce expert extraordinaire.

Hey. It's a much better gig than snapping bonds at the Wicked Wolf's whim. Punishing those who pissed him off by taking their mate from them. And, sure, I can only do that if there are any doubts—any cracks at all in the bond—but when the Alpha was threatening you, it's not surprising how quickly some mates fold. It takes a forever bond like the one between Gemma Swann and Ryker Wolfson—not to mention their alpha natures—to withstand that.

Roman wants to keep me on retainer, reserving my skill for his use only. I'm okay with that, especially when I saw how much he was willing to pay for the privilege.

I'm not a fool; at least, not when it comes to money. I've eaten out of dumpsters, slept in sketchy motels, and sold fortunes for pennies. Easy come, easy go... Roman Zakharov might be a better master than Wicked Wolf Walker, but either he'll tire of me or he'll want something I can't give him. Everyone does eventually. I can't get used to having this much money.

Doesn't mean that I'm going to hoard it. I went looking for a job in the first place because I knew that I had some expenses. Foods. Toiletries.

Clothes.

When I moved into Muncie, I only had a few changes of clothing that I carried in my duffel bag. Some old t-shirts, two pairs of jeans, a simple shift dress, and a couple of sets of cheap panties and bras. Enough to keep me covered, but nothing fancy.

And then I got my first paycheck and decided I deserved a tiny upgrade to my wardrobe.

I didn't go overboard. The dress code for working

under Roman is non-existent. I've seen Leigh dressed to the nines some days, while wearing jeans and a simple tee the next. It's the same with the other vampires that come and go in the building. So long as I'm decent, he doesn't care what I wear.

I got a few nicer sweaters, an extra pair of jeans, more luxurious undergarments—and a dress.

I didn't need it. There was no reason to buy it. But when I saw the sleeveless, fitted golden dress... I couldn't help myself. I tried it on, stunned at how well it molded to my curves. It barely covers my boobs, reaching to the middle of my thighs, but it looked so good on me, I couldn't stop myself from buying it. Plus the color... like how red is the color of vampires, gold belongs to the shifters. This dress was made for me, and it was the only thing I owned that was appropriate for a night out.

"You look hot," Gretchen says approvingly. "You'll fit right in at Mea Culpa."

"Um. Thanks."

"Don't mention it. Just stay close, and prepare to have the best night of your life. When you're with us, it's always a given."

CHAPTER 10

Despite Gretchen's boasting, I'm a little nervous as I follow the trio into the club. I keep expecting the bouncer to figure out I'm a shifter and tell me that I'm not allowed inside, but it seems like being buffered by three vampire females is all I need.

Mea Culpa is a supe club, no humans allowed. Of course, because I'm the only shifter in Muncie, I'm the only non-vampire inside. That catches a couple of curious club-goers' attention, but no one bothers me. It's like we all came here for a good time, and before long I begin to shed my nerves.

Until about an hour into our night out when, suddenly, I feel the familiar prickle of ice against the back of my neck.

Oh, no. Not now. Tell me Aleks isn't here *now*.

I turn behind me. And, yup. There he is. Standing on the edge of the dance floor where I'd been bopping along with Tamera and Leigh, Aleks is watching me with an unreadable expression.

One thing for sure? He isn't happy.

As our eyes meet across the floor, I immediately stop dancing. There's a hunger in his gaze that isn't as noticeable in the thin line of his lips. His eyes dip down to the low cut of my dress and his whole body goes tight. Then, before I can duck behind someone, he crosses his arms over his chest.

Oh, boy. I'm in trouble.

Tamera is the first one to notice that something is up. Following the direction of my stare, she frowns when she spies Aleks.

"What is he doing here? I thought Aleksander was on patrol tonight."

She glances over at Leigh.

Leigh nods. "Every night, from ten at night until six in the morning." Or, I think to myself, whenever he's not standing outside of my townhouse—or is that part of his patrol, too? "As far as I know, he's on schedule tonight. Roman didn't mention that someone was taking his shift."

And he would know, too, since every part of protecting the Fang City's borders goes through Roman.

Tamera's puzzled look turns to one of understanding. "Ah. I don't think he's here to dance, my beloved. I think he's here for his wolf."

I think she's right.

Leigh brushes against me. "You want us to get you out of here? Tamera can distract him and I can cover you while you go."

That's a tempting idea, but I never get the chance. Before we can escape the crowd on the dance floor, Aleks is already making a beeline straight for me.

I might as well meet him halfway.

"Thanks for the offer," I mumble, "but I should probably handle this myself."

Leigh murmurs a quick *good luck* while she and Tamera slip away, probably in search of Gretchen.

Taking a deep breath, I bring a smile to my face as I meet Aleks. "Hi. Didn't expect to see you here."

"Me, neither. What are you doing at this club?"

"Um. Dancing?"

Aleks doesn't like that. A hint of a growl underlines his accented voice as he tells me, "It's for vampires, and you don't have your fang."

"You mean the one you stole from me? Gee, Aleks. I wonder why not."

Ah, Luna. Why am I mouthing off to him? He's a powerful vampire, I'm a cursed wolf, and I've spent too many years being taught over and over again not to talk back. When it comes to Aleks, though? I don't know... it's like it's the *only* time I can fight back because, no matter what, he won't hurt me.

He promised.

I shake my head, tossing my hair over my shoulder. "Besides, I think I'm okay. I might not have the fang on me, but I'm not here alone."

"I know. You were dancing with another male."

Wait— was I? I didn't even notice. I thought I was dancing in a group, alongside Leigh and her blood-bonded mate, with Gretchen off getting a shot of O-negative from the bar.

"That's not what I meant. I was invited out by Leigh and her friends. She said I'd be safe with them even without the fang."

Aleks doesn't have a response for that. Instead, his light green eyes suddenly threading with red, he says, "Tell the other ladies goodnight. I'm taking you home."

"What? Already? I... I want to stay."

That's a lie. I've never been much of a club girl even when I was younger, and the sights and scents inside of Mea Culpa have made my wolf uncomfortable from the moment I entered behind Gretchen. The amount of vampires has her growling under her breath, and I don't blame her. I'm the only one in the whole club with a pulse. Something like that would make anyone leery.

But I'm not about to admit that to Aleks. He might be my fated mate, but I don't want him to get the idea that he can order me around. I mean, I *like* it. Letting him take control... it flips a switch inside of me, making him even more attractive—as if that was even possible. There should still be some element of a partnership between mates, though. He can tell me what to do, and I should feel free to tell him to shove it.

Not tonight, it seems. All Aleks says is, "No. You don't," before he lifts his hand, waving over to where Tamera and Leigh are now. He catches the redhead's eye, nodding down at me. She returns the nod, leaning to whisper something in Leigh's ear. Leigh's soft hazel eyes widen, but before she can start toward me, Aleks has his arm around my shoulder, guiding me through the throng of dancers.

No one even looks twice. They definitely don't try to interfere.

I wait until we're back outside before I shove his arm off of me. Satisfied that he whisked me out of the club, he lets me.

"What are you doing?" I demand.

"Keeping my beloved safe."

Yours, whispers the Luna.

I ignore her.

"I'm not your beloved."

"*Yet*."

Oh my Luna... he's got to be kidding me.

"I think I liked you better when you were pretending you didn't know who I was."

Aleks frowns. "I had my reasons."

Right. Just like I had my reasons to go along with it. "Remember them," I suggest. "Then we can go back to how it was."

"What if I don't want to?"

His gentle whisper seems to echo all around me. I shiver.

"You're cold," he observes. "Did you bring a coat? I can go back inside and retrieve it for you."

I'd rather wear a hundred coats than admit that I was shivering because of what he said.

I shake my head, letting my curtain of hair fall forward, covering my cleavage. "It's okay. Since you dragged me out of the club, I might as well just go home anyway. I'll be okay until then."

He immediately starts shrugging off his jacket. "Wear mine."

So he'll have an excuse to see me again to get it back? I'll wear a hundred coats—just not his. "No, thanks."

Aleks freezes, but I think he can tell that he's pushed me far enough tonight. "Are you sure?"

"Yes."

"Very well. If you change your mind on the walk, let me know." He pulls his coat back on. "Lead the way, Elizabeth."

"Excuse me?"

"I'm coming with you."

What? "Aren't you supposed to be on patrol?"

"Tak. But I'm also the reason you don't have protection. I'll walk you home so that I know you're safe then head back out."

"I'll be fine." When Aleks's eyes flash in the streetlight, I cut him off before he can argue with me. "I made it nearly thirty years without a bodyguard. Made it a couple of weeks before I started working for Roman. I've always been able to take care of myself on my own. Don't worry about me."

"Muszę, mój Elizabeth." Then, in a low voice, he adds, "You shouldn't have *had* to. I should've found you well before this."

Maybe. And maybe if he had, I wouldn't feel the need to reject him in order to save myself from more trouble.

"Goodnight, Aleks."

I turn, already walking away. If I don't, he might say the right thing, get me to stay. And I can't.

I *can't*.

He calls after me anyway. "Elizabeth. Wait."

Don't turn around. Don't turn ar—

I look over my shoulder. "Yes—*oh*."

He's right behind me, closing the gap between us. Reaching up, Aleks snaps the fang out of his mouth with a cracking sound that sends another round of shivers coursing down my spine.

"Before you go, take this."

Holding up my hands, I back away from him. "I... I can't."

"If you're worried that it won't grow back—"

"It's not that." I already know it will. Roman's did within two days.

"Then what is it, księżyca?"

I really need to find out what that means. Gem wasn't kidding when she said I'd need a Polish to English dictionary. My idiot self left it on my nightstand. At least I started practicing on the language app I downloaded, but so far all I've learned is how to count to ten, that 'tak' means 'yes', and that Roman's Russian is totally different than Aleks's Polish.

"Roman gave me a fang to wear so that no one would bother me in Muncie. If I take yours, what would that mean?"

His eyes flash beneath the growing moonlight. "Ah. You've been talking to Gem."

I don't deny it. "She's told me a lot about you."

I could've meant anything by that. She lived with Aleks for more than a year before Ryker tracked her down and made his move, so there's plenty she could have shared.

Then Aleks frowns, and I know that *he* knows exactly what I'm talking about.

"I make no excuses for my pursuit of her. I spent two hundred years believing I'd never have a beloved to call my own after Julia was... gone, and when a female alpha appeared at the borders all those years later, I believed I found her. Of course, then I saw you, and I knew that it wasn't a female alpha I was waiting for, but"—he gestures with his hand toward my eyes—"one with the mark of the Luna."

So... he knows what the silver color of my eyes means, huh? Looks like I'm not the only one who's been talking to Gem.

"Did you love her?"

I can't believe that just popped out of my mouth. The second it does, though, I realize that I need to know. He obviously still loves his Julia, but what about Gem?

"I love her still, but not the way you think, księżyca."

I wait for Aleks to elaborate. When he doesn't, I ask simply, "Is that true?"

"Can't you tell?" When I shake my head, he says, "Gem could sense when someone was lying to her."

"I'm not Gem."

"No," Aleks agrees easily, "you're not. And you're not Julia, either. You're Elizabeth."

I nod at the fang nestled in his palm. "And you still want me to take that?"

"Tak. Because you're *my* Elizabeth."

I want so badly to believe that he *is* telling the truth.

But I can't. Not yet. Not while I can't shake the

belief that, when he looks at me, he sees someone I'm not. That I can never be.

My lips part. At first, it's a sigh, then it's the beginning of another rejection—but I don't get that far.

Moving into me, Aleks cups my nape, tilting my head back.

Our eyes lock.

At this moment, I know that he could easily take my mouth if he wanted to. I couldn't stop him. Deep down, I know I wouldn't even if I could.

He waits, searching for permission.

Parting my lips further, I give it to him.

It's been years since I've been kissed. I avoided any and all male attention in the district pretty well. No one wanted to go up against the Alpha, and even someone like Brendan, who showed interest, never shows it for long. I guard myself carefully when I'm playing at being a human, so that never worked. Before that, I was so scarred after what happened with Kyle and Peyton, I couldn't risk a repeat of starting an affair with the wrong male.

Aleks is wrong for me in so many ways. I need a mate who will put me first, who will help heal a decade's worth of loneliness. With the vampire, I know I'll never get past being his second—or even his *third*—choice. He's pursuing me now because he believes I'm his beloved, his fated mate, and that I owe it to him to surrender.

As his lips brush gently against mine, the beginning of a kiss that turns probing, then demanding a heartbeat later, I try so hard not to. It'll only lead to heartache in the end, but... *Luna*... this male is the best kisser I've ever known.

He has his right hand cupping my neck. Folding his left hand into a fist, holding tightly to the fang, he rests it against the small of my back. He's holding me upright, leaving me to do just what I didn't want to.

I surrender to his claiming kiss.

His tongue slides against mine. I follow his lead, lapping at his, avoiding the point of his remaining fang. There's no lingering taste of blood in his mouth. It's fresh and it's clean and I clutch my hands against his chest, pulling him closer.

He doesn't need to breathe, but I do. Eventually breaking the kiss, Aleks bows his body over me, trailing his soft lips against the column of my neck. When his chin nuzzles the point where it meets my shoulder, I suddenly remember where I am—and who I'm with.

I stiffen.

He's not going to bite me again, is he?

Trailing a line with his only fang, he doesn't break the skin. "If you won't wear it close to your heart," he murmurs into my hair when he's done, "then at least place it in your pocket. It'll give you nearly as much protection as Roman's, and I need you to be safe. In time, I'll earn your neck again—and your heart."

Something tells me that Aleks isn't just talking about me wearing a golden chain around my neck, his fang hanging over my heart.

"Okay," I say breathlessly. Pulling away from him, putting as much space between us as my wolf will allow, I hold out my hand. "I'll take the fang."

He presses it against my palm.

Aleks's fingers are chilled. So, tell me, why am I burning up again from that one last touch?

It's times like these that I wonder why, when I go from skin to fur, my other half is a white wolf. If my animal truly represented what I was, I should be a giant fucking chicken.

I'm a coward. I hate it, but it is what it is. As soon as I left Aleks outside of Mea Culpa, I made a break for home. I didn't shift, though I did kick off my heels about a block into my journey back. I wasn't so desperate that I was going to call for a ride when, normally, the distance between the club and my home was nothing for me and my wolf, but I move a lot faster without the shoes. It was bad enough I was already slowed down by my dress. I couldn't walk the streets of Muncie naked without drawing attention, but hopefully none of the humans I met realized I was barefoot.

After that, I didn't leave the townhouse again. And if I sensed him out there? I kept my shades drawn so that I didn't tease my lonely wolf with glimpses of him.

On Monday, though, it was time to return to work. I had hoped that I could put my last conversation with Aleks behind me. That I could forget all about him.

Yeah... that lasted until I stepped outside my front door and discovered that someone had recovered my heels and propped them up neatly on the porch.

Someone.

Right.

It had to be Aleks. By Monday, his scent wasn't as strong as it would've been Friday night, but I've become so much more sensitive to it lately. Was it because of his fang in my pocket? Maybe. Or because I fed him my blood. Either way, he's the one who saved my shoes which means he must have followed me home that night.

Keeping watch over me, just like he told Roman he would.

I don't know what to think about it. So I do what I always do: I don't. I pretend I don't notice, scurrying past them, making my way to the center of town all while hoping that I don't run into him.

From what I understand, Aleks is one of the vampires who gets his rest during the day. Because

Muncie is a Fang City, the more powerful Cadre members devote their attention to the night. That's why Aleks's patrol runs from ten to six, and why he always seems to visit the townhouse while I'm sleeping.

It's another reason why I was always able to avoid him during the day—until he decided to start checking in on me at the Cadre building while I was working.

Claws crossed that he doesn't today.

CHAPTER 11

By Thursday, I've decided I'm not just a chicken. I'm also a *hypocrite*.

Aleks hasn't stopped by the Cadre building all week. I caught a hint of his scent lingering near the townhouse on Tuesday, but we've had a bit of an unseasonably warm spell. It hasn't snowed in days—and any slush and ice lingering has long since melted—so there was no way for me to check to see if he left any prints behind on my sidewalk.

It's like he disappeared. He called me his beloved, gave me his fang, and now he's gone.

He's waiting for you to go to him, the Luna whispers. *He doesn't know you long for the chase.*

How could he? He's a vampire. He doesn't know how to participate in the mating dance, not the way a shifter would, and it's driving me nuts that—despite rejecting him—my shifter side needs him to come after me to prove he's serious in his pursuit.

And Aleks? It seems like he's giving me my space. Either that, or he's decided I'm not worth the hassle.

I don't know what's worse, and by Thursday, I almost want to call Aleks just to hear his aristocratic voice.

I blame Gem. After my last visit to Accalia, I realized I didn't just leave with the dictionary. Oh, no. Somehow, she got her paws on my phone, entering Aleks's phone number into my meager list of contacts.

She even put the blood drop emoji, followed by the heart emoji next to his name, in case I knew a million other Aleks's and I needed to differentiate.

I had half a mind to erase it. If only to get rid of any temptation, my finger hovered over the delete button before I decided against it. After all, Aleks is a high-ranking member of the Cadre. It might not be a bad idea to have a way to contact him in an emergency.

Though Aleks might not be visiting the receptionist desk, that doesn't mean that no one has. Thursday evening, just before the end of my shift, Gretchen came by to flirt with Leigh again.

On the one hand, I finally discovered who Leigh and Tamera were hoping to make their third. On the other, the iridescent vampire seems to have decided to make me her pet project.

Emphasis on the *pet* part.

Gretchen leans against the counter, her blonde hair spilling over one shoulder as she glances down at me. "You're coming with us this weekend. We'll have a re-do of last Friday, and hope that Aleksander doesn't act like a spoilsport again."

If there's one thing I've learned since living among vampires—especially those who are part of the Cadre in one way or another—it's that they never *ask* for anything. They demand, and they expect to be obeyed as if it was their due.

"Maybe," I say, giving her a non-committal answer.

"What's the matter, wolfy? You had fun the other night with us fangers, right?"

Fun. I guess you could call all that unresolved sexual tension I dealt with later *fun*—if you were a sadist.

"Gretchen. Leave Elizabeth alone. She doesn't have to come if she doesn't want to."

Gretchen sniffs. "Is it because she traded Roman's fang for Aleksander's? A bit of a downgrade, power-wise, but I get it. He is much prettier than Roman."

"Oh my god, Gretchen." Leigh casts her eyes to the ceiling, nibbling nervously on her bottom lip. "You know that Roman probably heard that, right?"

Most likely. There are cameras in nearly every corner of the Cadre building. I can't decide if Roman is paranoid, or just very particular when it comes to security. I'm leaning toward a mix of options A and B. Any good leader does what it takes to keep his people safe, but even I think constant patrols and perimeter checks around Muncie's borders might be a tad bit overkill.

Do I think he watches what goes on in this building? Definitely. Does he have the mikes on? I doubt it, but that doesn't mean he can't flick the switch to listen in whenever he wants.

Gretchen's not wrong, though. Aleks is prettier than Roman—not that I'll ever admit that out loud where it could be used against me later on.

I don't even bother asking how she knows I have Aleks's fang. Just like how Leigh was the first to sense it when Roman's was gone, it had to be obvious that I had another one in my possession—and exactly what overprotective vampire would have been the one to give it to me.

Tossing her long blonde hair over her shoulder, Gretchen says to Leigh, "So? You guys work for the Cadre. I don't. Besides, we all know that Roman rarely gives out one of his fangs while Aleks makes a habit of it. It doesn't mean anything—"

Leigh slaps the front of the counter with the flat of her hand. "Gretch!"

"What? Again, you know I'm right. Everyone in Muncie knows about his wolf fetish." With a royal look my way, she adds almost flippantly, "No offense."

The worst part? She actually means that. She's not trying to be rude. Gretchen just comes off that way.

Besides, she isn't wrong. When it comes to Aleks's wolf fetish, I'm more than aware of it. Just like how I've had more details about Gem's run-in with my new friends.

Over the last weekend, I checked in with her. I let her know that something was brewing down here in the Fang City, and she gave me a little more detail about the two vampires who ambushed me. Turns out that, while she lived in Muncie, she had more than a couple of altercations with vampires who were plotting against Roman. It was actually Ryker who killed Stefan when he targeted Gem, while Roman executed Monroe for selling his fang to Ryker's former Beta, Shane. The Wicked Wolf had been calling the shots back then; now that I've had some time to think about it, I'm terrified that he's doing the same thing now.

Sure, we could give a dog to another...

It will weaken him to throw her back to the wolves...

Because I figured I had no choice, I also told her about the two who came after me. Aleks handled Hector when he tried to lunge at me, fangs bared, but Anton is missing and could still be a threat. I might not be a member of the Mountainside Pack, but Gem has my personal loyalty. In case it didn't get back to her and Ryker already, I wanted her to know.

She thanked me, then—in pure alpha fashion—ordered me to bunker down in the townhouse where I was safe. She even offered to send me one of her guards again, but I gently refused.

Why bother when I have a vampire of my own watching over me?

I also let slip that I had visited Mea Culpa with Leigh, her mate, and the blonde vampire. Like I thought, she wasn't happy, though she was impressed that I made friends with them without any of the Nightmare Trio going for my throat first.

And I guess we are friends, as strange as that seems. If not friends, then *friendly,* but still. It's a start.

When six o'clock comes, Gretchen is still trying to convince me that I should give the club a second try. Promising her I'll think about it, I say goodbye to her and Leigh, grab my coat and my purse, then head on out.

February in Muncie means that it's already dark at six o'clock. I don't really mind. With Aleks's fang in my pocket, I feel comfortable walking around the city again. I can flash it if any vampire wants to give me trouble, and if it's a human? I might not be as strong as one of the higher ranked wolves, but even a Luna-touched shifter like me can handle a human no problem.

I have a couple of errands to run. They barely take a half an hour, and by quarter to seven I'm just strolling down the street that would lead me home.

There's about a two-block radius surrounding the

townhouse that I consider my territory. When I reach it, it's almost instinctive. I breathe in deep, tasting scents, making sure that it's just as I left it when I head off to work this morning.

Tonight, it isn't.

At first, I can't put my finger on it. Pausing on the corner, my wolf's hackles rising, I reach out with my senses. When I butt up against a territorial marking that isn't mine, my heart starts to pound.

My reaction is instantaneous. Without even realizing what I'm doing, I reach inside my bag, trembling fingers finding my phone. It takes two tries to select my contacts list.

Aleks starts with A. It's at the top of the list.

I call him, torn between the need to reinforce my territory and a decade's long habit of running away at the first sign of trouble.

Your mate will know what to do.

I really fucking hope so.

On the second ring, he answers. "Who is this? How did you get this number?"

He sounds so annoyed, I almost hang up. If it wasn't for the Luna's advice, I might have.

Instead, I whisper, "Gem gave it to me. I... I hope it's okay."

His attitude changes in a heartbeat.

"Księżyca? What's wrong?"

I don't know. How can I tell him when I'm not so

sure? Especially after it's been a week since I spoke to him last, and now I'm calling him for help?

It seems right, though, like he's the only one I *could* go to for this.

"I... it's my house. Someone's here." No. The scent markers are old. "They were here. I think they're gone now." Another tentative sniff, reinforcing my first opinion. "Shifters," I tell him. "It's a wolf. I'm not sure who, but it's definitely a wolf."

"Did you tell Roman?"

It never even occurred to me to do that. "No. You're the first one I called."

"Wait for me," Aleks orders. "Don't go inside until I arrive."

I want to remind him that I'm a shifter, too. That I have no idea why I reached out to him when I'm more than capable of protecting my own territory.

He's used to alpha females. Julia. Gem. Neither one of them would take his dominance without a fight.

But that's the thing. I'm not an alpha. If it wasn't for my family's curse, I'd probably top out at a maternal delta—or, worse, a feral scavenger. I'm too selfish to be an omega, and too weak to be a beta.

There's only one thing I can do right now.

"Okay." Nodding to myself since he can't see me, I tell him, "I'll wait."

I don't know where he came from. It's not even seven yet, so I doubt he started his overnight patrol, but wherever he was, I sense the approach of his powerful aura while I'm still working up the nerve to call Gem and let her know that someone sprayed around the outside of her old townhouse.

It's a territorial marking. Our animal instincts lead us to do it, though it's usually when the wolf's in control. At some point tonight, an oversized wolf was prowling the streets of Muncie in time to piss all over my porch before doing Luna only knows what.

If this isn't some kind of declaration, I don't know what is.

Thanks to my wolf, I sense Aleks before I see him. His aura is a gentle caress, warmer than the evening breeze; it carries the promise of snow in its chill. It's so strange that the undead vampire with the cold touch and the icy skin can have any kind of warmth. Of course, then I remember how hot his lips felt against mine when he kissed me and I guess it makes some sense.

His aura first, then his scent. Something about Aleks is unique. Each vampire has a similar base—the previously dead before rising again part—but his has a kind of unusual spice that belongs to only him. Fennel, maybe, or a very faint licorice aroma. You have to be in tune with him to notice it, and after all those nights he stood outside of my townhouse, it's ingrained in my memory.

Is that why the unknown shifter pissed outside of my house? To erase it?

I really hope not.

When Aleks appears in my line of vision, I stumble a few steps in his direction.

He races toward me, wrapping me up in his arms when he's near enough. I don't fight the embrace even though my first instinct is to push him away. Aleks might have finally decided that he's all in on me, but I still haven't.

Not yet, at least.

His body against mine is tight. Thrumming. As I pull back, I notice that his eyes are red in an instant.

"Aleks?"

"*Blood*."

I shiver. "What's that?"

"The street reeks of it. Freshly spilled." Pausing for a moment, he says in a deadly tone, "Vampire's blood."

I blink. "You're kidding."

He shakes his head.

I must've gone nose-blind in Muncie; either that, or I've been too complacent. The scent of blood is to be expected in a Fang City. The dark miasma that rubbed my fur the wrong way is what caught my attention, plus the wolfish notes mixed in with it.

And, you know. The piss. Can't forget about that.

"Did you go inside?"

"No. Not yet."

He eyes my front door before looking down at me again. "What are my chances of getting you to stay out here while I go and check it out?"

Smart vampire. Gem must've trained him well because that's definitely the sort of question one would ask a dominant female shifter.

"Honestly?" Despite how freaked out I am... "Zero."

This is my territory. I'm worried, but I'm also determined.

Aleks nods. Releasing me, he starts toward the door, but not before saying, "Stay close. I'll go first."

That works for me.

The door is unlocked. When Aleks notices that, he asks me if I left it that way. My answer is an emphatic *no*. Maybe in the Wolf District it was habit to leave doors open, but not in a Fang City. I lock up every time I leave, and something tells me that Aleks already knew that.

He pauses, fingers curled around the knob. "And you won't stay outside?" he double-checks.

"No."

He huffs, then pushes the door in.

The stench of spilled blood punches both of us. If it was bad on the street, it's a million times worse inside. Aleks immediately throws his arm up, as if he can shield me from it. I choke, then cough, trying to get past the worst of it.

Because, mingled with the blood, is a scent I know all too well.

Wolf.

And it's all coming from the second floor.

"Upstairs," I tell him.

He nods. "I know. I'm still going first."

"You do that. But I'll be right behind you."

He already thinks I'm some damsel in distress that needs to be saved—and maybe I am—but I'm not going to leave him to search the rest of the townhouse alone. If he's going up there, I'm going with him.

Even if I do keep a few steps behind him.

As soon as we reach the second floor, it's obvious where the source of the scent is coming from.

My bedroom.

To say that there's blood everywhere inside my personal space is an understatement. It's splashed on the wall, pooling in puddles on the floor, staining the quilt and the sheets on the bed a vivid scarlet. It's fresh, still shiny and wet, and it's so pungent that my wolf covers her snout with her paws. I do the same with my human hands and nose.

It doesn't help. The scent of blood covers everything—and I know exactly who it belongs to.

Anton.

His savaged body is thrown in one corner, but his

head… someone has propped his head up on my pillow.

My *pillow*.

Next to it, there's a folded note.

While I zero in on that, Aleks goes right to Anton's head. Using his thumb, he peels back the vampire's lip.

Anton is missing his right fang.

"Cholera."

I had already unfolded the note when Aleks spat out the word. It's not the disease he means, but *damn* in Polish. Even if I didn't know the difference, the way he spits out the word makes it pretty obvious it's a curse.

Right then, I'm on the same page with him. I hadn't had the chance to read what's written on the paper yet, but the three W's scrawled at the bottom? I know exactly who it's from.

A dead vampire with a missing fang, and a note from the former Alpha of the Western Pack? You don't need to be a genius to put two and two together and get four.

Walker hates bloodsuckers, but he has no problem allying with them—or betraying them. And though it's not his wolfish scent that covers this room, hiding just beneath the reek of freshly spilled vampire blood, I have no doubt in my mind that this was done on his orders.

The note proves it.

While Aleks focuses on Anton's remains, I pick up

the paper. It's splattered with blood, the words printed by hand in a rich black ink.

It says:

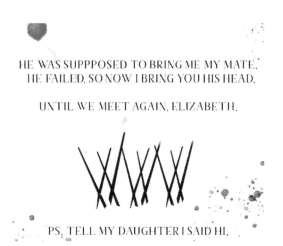

HE WAS SUPPPOSED TO BRING ME MY MATE.
HE FAILED, SO NOW I BRING YOU HIS HEAD.

UNTIL WE MEET AGAIN, ELIZABETH.

PS. TELL MY DAUGHTER I SAID HI.

Elizabeth. There goes any hope that this message—the broken door, the blood all over, *the vampire head in my bed*—was for Gem instead of me. *My mate...*

I'm not his mate. *My* mate is standing on the other side of the bed, glaring down at Anton's head, nostrils flaring almost imperceptibly as if tracing other scents. Anton's blood is the most prevalent, followed by the unknown shifter who slaughtered him. Then there's mine, and, of course, Gem's and Ryker's.

But that's not all. Centered on the note in my hand, there's a scent I hoped I'd never breathe into my lungs again.

Jack Walker's. It's all over the page. Even if he didn't

sign it—three heavily lined W's for the Wicked Wolf of the West—I would know exactly who it's from by the dark scent alone.

Clenching the page with trembling fingers, I start to shake.

Oh, no. No, no, no. This can't be happening.

Aleks sneaks up behind me, moving soundlessly to my side. "What do you have there, Elizabeth?"

I jump, then stupidly shove the paper behind my back. Right. Like that's going to stop Aleks from getting his hands on it if he really wants to know what I'm holding.

When he raises both of his eyebrows at me, I know his thoughts are along the same line as mine.

I sigh. "It's a note." A moment's pause. "From the Wicked Wolf."

"Jack Walker."

Aleks hates the Alpha. I knew that already. Why wouldn't he? But the expression of pure menace and loathing that shadows Aleks's beautiful face is a stark reminder that he can be as vicious with his enemies as he is careful with me.

I'm staring. I know I am. And I can't tell if I like this other side of Aleks—or if I want to bolt.

I think he can tell. Keeping his voice soft, he asks, "May I see it?"

"Uh. Yeah. Let me just..."

Pulling my phone out of my back pocket, I swipe

up, opening the camera app. Centering the note so that I have the whole thing in the screen, I snap a picture, then hand it over to Aleks. I know that once he has it, I won't see it again, and the threat scrawled on the paper doesn't just affect me.

While Aleks scans the few lines on the paper, I'm already searching for her contact in my meager list.

"He calls you his mate."

"I'm not," I say firmly.

"What are you doing?"

"Calling Gem."

For a moment, Aleks looks like he's about to argue with me. Wiping his hands on his pants, he turns away from me. "You should do that. The Alpha will need to be informed."

Right. And, courtesy of the note at the bottom, so does his mate.

I select her name, purposely giving Aleks—and the vampire head—my back as I wait for her to answer.

"Hello?"

I shift my phone so that the receiver is at my mouth again. "Gem. Hi. It's Elizabeth."

"Hey." The suspicion lacing her tone when she answered immediately fades. "What's up?"

I immediately launch into the most basic explanation. About how someone broke into her apartment, making a huge disaster of her old home, before I read her the note in my hand and she understands exactly who was behind the breach.

When Gem goes eerily quiet, digesting everything I said, Aleks holds out his hand. He waits expectantly for the phone.

I give it to him.

Lifting it to his ear, he greets Gem with another Polish phrase. "Mały wilku."

"Aleks. I'm heading to the den right now to get Ryker. We can be at the townhouse in twenty."

His lips thin. I know there's no love lost between him and Gem's mate, but this is the first time I'm seeing it. "Better not. Anton might've been one of the rebels, but he was a vampire. This is a Cadre problem."

"What about Elizabeth?"

Good question, Gem. What about me?

"She will be protected."

"Oh. That's right. She has Zakharov's fang."

Not anymore, Gem. Of course, she doesn't know that, though, and he doesn't tell her otherwise.

I wonder why.

They talk for a few seconds more before Aleks ends the call. When he offers me my phone back, I accept it.

"I'm going to call Roman," he tells me, pulling out his own phone. "Let him know what we found. While I do, pack everything you're going to need. You can't stay here tonight."

You will be protected, the Luna whispers. It's exactly

what Aleks said to Gem, but hearing it from my goddess has me frowning over at him.

"Where will I go?" Gem would welcome me. I know she would. "Accalia?"

"No."

Okay.

"Then where?"

With a look that dares me to defy him, Aleks says, "To my home. Now pack your bags, Elizabeth. You won't be coming back here for a while."

Then, before I do anything but blink up at him in surprise, Aleks walks out of the room.

I shake my head, just a touch stunned. And, if I'm being honest, a little turned on; the submissive wolf inside of me has always responded to a male more dominant than I am. Then, trying not to read too much into his command, I head over to my closet, yanking out the empty duffle bag I have stowed in there.

It's time to pack.

CHAPTER 12

Aleks holds the door to his twelfth-floor apartment open for me.

"Thank you," I murmur.

"Nie ma za co."

You're welcome.

Look at that. I'm getting better at recognizing some phrases—and not just the curse words. Score one for the language app on my phone.

Holding the strap of my duffel bag to my chest, I walk into Aleks's apartment for the first time. The entrance leads directly into a stylishly decorated living room complete with a cream-colored settee, a glass-topped coffee table, and a huge screen television mounted on the wall. The kitchen is off to my right. Moving further in, I see the hall that will lead to the bathroom and the bedrooms, plus the wide glass sliding door that opens to the balcony outside.

I think it's beautiful. Exactly the sort of space I'd expect Aleks to have, and I'd be giddy over finally seeing it if it wasn't for one teensy, tiny thing: it smells like Gem in here.

I thought I was prepared for that. I'm not.

She's been gone since last summer, but her scent still lingers. The only way I can get through this is by remembering what she said. They were roommates—platonic roommates. She had her own room, and Aleks had his.

Right now, I can't say for sure that I know what's going on between me and Aleks. Little more than a week ago, we were strangers. Since then, I've fed him my blood, kissed him, taken his fang, and now I'm staying with him because some sick shifter left a vampire's head in my bedroom.

I'm fucking exhausted. I'm beginning to think that I might have been better off grabbing my tarot cards and the cash Roman's given me already and getting the heck out of Dodge. Since that option is currently off the table, I'm going to bed. Maybe eat something. I always do my best thinking on a full stomach.

But, first, I'm putting this bag down. Aleks tried to convince me to let him carry it, but the stubborn side of me that rarely rears its head had refused. It's not heavy, not for a shifter, but I'd still feel better putting it down.

Following the scent trail, I start down the hall.

"Where are you going, Elizabeth?" he calls after me.

I point at the farthest door. "That one is Gem's room, right?"

He nods.

"I was going to put my bag in there, then figure out what to eat."

As bad as the scene in the townhouse was, I still have my appetite. When I was on the run—even when I was trapped in the district—I had to go hungry more often than not; either because I was low on funds, or because I didn't want to give any male the wrong idea. Now? I eat what I want, when I want, and I'm starving.

'That's fine. But don't put your bag in that room." Shifting on his heel, he points toward the first closed door at the beginning of the hall. "Put it in there."

"Whose room is that?" I ask, even though I'm pretty sure I already know.

I'm right.

"It's mine." His lips thin into a fine line as he meets me in the middle of the hall. "While you're here, you'll be sleeping in that room."

I will? "Aleks... maybe it's better that I take the couch then."

Tucking his finger under my chin, he tilts my

head enough so that I'm forced to meet his steely gaze. His irises are still a gentle soft green, but I know that it won't take much for me to make them turn red.

"You won't wear my fang near your heart," he grates out, his accent growing more noticeable. "Won't you at least sleep in my bed?"

"Aleks, I—"

"You need your rest. I aim to make sure you get it. I'll sleep elsewhere."

"Where?"

"Excuse me?"

"Where are you going to sleep?"

If I'm in his bed, and he doesn't want to sleep next to me, would he use Gem's old bed instead?

The idea that he would bothers me more than it should. I have no right to be jealous, and yet there are two females I can't measure up to. One is dead, the other happily mated, and then there's me.

Maybe I *should* leave Muncie while I can...

"If you're not comfortable sharing," he says after a moment's pause, "I will take the couch."

It's not a matter of being comfortable. With the Luna only a week from being full, it's more that I'm afraid I'll lose control around him.

I have before. And, despite everything being so unsettled between us, I'm sure I will again.

"You don't have to make a decision now, though,"

he adds. Turning toward the kitchen he says, "You're hungry. I'll go make some dinner for you."

Alarm bells go off inside of my head at just how smoothly he offered to do so.

In shifter culture, making food for—or providing it to—a prospective mate has a very specific meaning. It means: *I will protect you, I will feed you, and you'll want for nothing if I'm around*. If I eat it, I'm basically saying *sure*.

"Point me to the kitchen. If you don't mind, I can fend for myself."

"You liked it when I cooked for you before."

I did, but that was before everything else happened. Before he so fiercely ripped Roman's necklace from my throat, replacing it with the one I have in my pocket right now. Before a similar fierceness replaced his usually gentlemanly facade tonight, giving me no choice but to follow him home.

He's acting too much like a possessive, bonded shifter for me to feel comfortable eating another of his meals when he doesn't know what it means to me and my wolf.

"Shouldn't you be on patrol?"

Aleks shakes his head. "Not tonight. When I called Roman, he passed my full-turn onto a quarter-turn patroller. Sonya is looking to rise within the Cadre. She'll take the chance to prove herself to Roman, and I have the night to spend with my beloved."

He sounds like he means it, too. Like having a few hours with me is all he wants.

I can't take it anymore.

Because honestly? I kind of want that, too, and if it turns out that we were both fooling ourselves all along, I'm not sure I'll survive his rejection. Even worse, I have the Alpha to worry about now.

Until we meet again, Elizabeth.

If the Wicked Wolf is regarding me as his, I'd hate to see what he does to Aleks when he finds out that the vampire he tortured truly is my fated mate.

The only way to keep him safe from the Wicked Wolf is by pushing him away from me, no matter how much it hurts.

I want him, but I still can't have him—and he needs to know that.

"You don't have to do that."

He frowns. "What am I doing wrong, Elizabeth? How can I show you that I can be a good mate to you if you won't let me?"

Wait... is that what he's trying to do? That's supposed to be a shifter thing, not a vampire courting ritual.

Then again, I *am* a shifter. And maybe Aleks is trying to appeal to me and my wolf by acting the way he would if he was the same.

Ah, Luna... we're in the middle of the mating dance, aren't we?

With the threat of the Alpha renewed, Peyton's sudden reappearance after a seven-year absence, and the reminder of his first beloved still lurking in that back of mind, that is quite possibly the *last* thing I need right now.

"Aleks, I..."

I *what*?

"Gem told me that feeding you would show your wolf that I'm a good male. A good provider. You must be hungry. Let me feed you."

"Gem said that?"

He nods.

I bite back my scowl.

Next time I talk to her again, I'll have to ask her why she's giving Aleks tips to court me. I thought she was on *my* side.

I should say no. Accepting food from Aleks, knowing full well his intentions behind it now... I should say no.

But I don't.

Hefting up my duffel bag, I rest my hand on the doorknob to Aleks's room. "Okay. Let me put the bag down and I'll join you in the kitchen."

HE COOKED FOR ME, BUT THE MANNERS INSTILLED IN ME from puphood have me insisting on clearing the table and washing up. He joins me, insisting in turn that he be allowed to grab a dishcloth so that he can help. It isn't until we're done that I realize just how... *domestic* the scene was.

Aleks is in a much better mood after dinner. He obviously feels as if he's won one small battle in the war between us by getting me to eat his food. If you ask me, I came out ahead since Aleks, for all that he doesn't eat human food regularly, is a pretty good cook.

He chats amicably about anything and everything —he tells me about the latest thriller he's reading before changing the subject to how the patrols around Muncie work—while I can't get past the fact that this is what life would be like if I ever bonded fully to Aleks.

I'm still dwelling on that when he asks if I'm ready to turn in for bed. Over dinner, I pointed out how ridiculous it would be for him to take the couch. I'm twenty-nine, he's... *older*. We're both mature adults. If we can't sleep in bed together without issue, there won't be any hope for me as his beloved.

Was it a manipulative move? At the time, I didn't think so. As Aleks strips down to his boxers, taking the left side of the bed, I begin to second-guess my intentions. I've already used the bathroom to brush my teeth, wash my face, and change into a t-shirt and sweatpants. It's what I usually wear to go to bed, but when he catches sight of me inching my way into the room, you would've thought I was wearing the finest lingerie.

He looks so... so *hungry*.

I can't get his expression out of my head. Even after he switches off the light, the two of us laying together in his king-sized bed, I still see it.

Turning on my side, giving Aleks my back, I begin to think that the couch might have been the better option after all.

In the quiet of the room, his voice seems to echo. "Elizabeth? Is everything okay?"

"Yeah. I'm just thinking."

That much, at least, is true.

"Thinking about what?"

"It's stupid."

He edges a little closer to me. His fingers reach out, caressing my hand. It's a reminder that, though it's dark, we're both supes. We don't need the light to see each other clearly. "I'm sure it isn't. Come, księżyca. Tell me."

"It's just... you didn't eat. I did, but you didn't have anything but tea."

"Ah." How can he make that single sound say so much? "You're worried about me? You want to take care of me, too? Is that it, my beloved?"

I want to tell him that he's way off base. That I'm not his beloved.

But those would be lies. And even if this ends up

being one big mistake, it doesn't feel right lying to my mate.

"I…"

"Yes?"

Does he know what I *really* want to say? Something tells me that he does, that he's waiting for me to find a way to articulate it to him.

Oh, Luna. Why is this so embarrassing? Before Aleks, I had a good amount of lovers. Before the Luna's touch made me wary of touching others, I enjoyed many males so that I could learn all about pleasure before I met the one meant specifically for me. Kyle might have been the last, so I've had a seven-year-long dry spell, but you'd think I was a skittish virgin the way I can't tell Aleks what I want from him.

I want *him*. I might not be able to claim him, but I want to show him my appreciation for everything he's done for me lately. And, hey, if I get some pleasure out of it… it seems like a win-win to me.

I swallow, grateful for the darkness in his room as I blurt out, "You can bite me again. I mean, if you want. If you're hungry."

The silken sheets rustle as Aleks slides closer to me. The chill of his skin is a balm against my embarrassment; the erection poking into the small of my back is a sure sign that he has some idea what I'm thinking.

"Would it frighten you, mój księżyca, if I told you that being near you... you make me starved for you?"

The way his voice drops to a whisper like that? When I shiver, fear is the last thing I'm feeling.

"Not at all."

"What if I told you that I'd do anything for a taste?"

I gulp. His cock pushes against me, but I inch even closer to Aleks. "Then I'd tell you that you're free to do so."

"You mean it?"

"I'm not in the habit of saying things I don't mean."

I can just about hear Aleks's slow grin when he says, "That's good to know."

My back is to him. I can't see what he's doing, but I can sense him as he moves. The memory of the pleasure from just the other night has me getting wet already. Clenching my thighs together, I slide my head on the pillow giving him access to my neck.

Only... that's not where Aleks touches me.

To my shock, he pulls the blanket covering us off before resting his hand on my hip. With a gentle tug, he eases me onto my back. As I let out a small gasp, he slips his hand between my thighs. The push he gives them is a little firmer, forcing them apart.

Once he has, he climbs over my leg, settling his shoulders in the cradle of my body.

"What... what are you doing?" It comes out breathless. "Aleks?"

"You told me I could have a taste. Did you not?" His fingers hook in the waistband of my sweatpants. "Up," he orders. I immediately lift my ass off of the bed. He shimmies the sweatpants down, taking my panties with them. "Elizabeth?"

Is he talking to me? I'm too distracted watching the way he's scooted down the bed, giving him room to tug one leg of my pants off, then the next. Before I know it, I'm completely naked from the waist down, and Aleks is looking at my revealed pussy like he's just found heaven.

Returning to his position between my legs, he blows a stream of cool breath on the top of my mound. "I said, did you not, Elizabeth?"

Did I not *what*? "Huh?"

"I told you I was starved. Now, your blood is divine. I promise you that. But I've had teases of your true scent these last few days and, to put it mildly, they've driven me nearly mad. To have you in my bed? To scent you growing wet for me? I'm starved, księżyca. This"—he runs the tips of three fingers down my slick folds— "is all I want to eat tonight. May I?"

He's so close to pleading, I can hardly believe it. This god of a vampire begging to eat me out?

"What did I say before?" I ask him.

Another caress. "I recall something like 'you're free to do so'."

"And what else?"

"That you always say what you mean."

"Then what do you think?"

He doesn't answer me. At least, not with words.

Holding me open with two fingers, Aleks nips at my clit before using the flat of his tongue to swipe up the length of my whole pussy.

I wiggle. I can't help it. That one lick feels so damn good that I want to get closer to his mouth. My flesh is hot, and his cool vampiric mouth is fucking *amazing*.

With a gentle slap to my clit, Aleks admonishes me. "Don't move, Elizabeth. For once, I have you right where I want you. Can you do that? I'll make it worth your while."

The wicked promise in his voice makes me want to do anything he says. "I'll try."

"That's my female." Another lick with a little more pressure this time. When I don't move, he goes back. Before I know it, he's doing exactly what he promised. He's tasting me every which way he can, and, yes, he definitely makes it worth my while even though I can't keep from squirming for long.

When I whimper that I need something more, Aleks slips a finger inside of me, giving my muscles something to tighten around as he dedicates everything else he has to my clit. My hands fist the sheets before he takes a quick break to tell me that he wants me to touch him.

And I do. I caress his neck, holding him close to

me. I remember being grateful that, as a vampire, he doesn't need to breathe, because I lose track of how long I ride his face. Eventually, my fingers end up threaded through his curls. They're so soft, the texture has me clinging to him just as I begin to come.

As I finally start to wind down from my climax, Aleks lowers himself further down my trembling body until he's nuzzling my inner thigh. I'm glad. My clit is so sensitized right now, if he went back for another lick, I'd have to shove him away from my pussy. My thigh, though? I can handle the jolt of pleasure his cool tongue gives me as he laves my skin.

And that's when he bites me, sucking on my thigh, taking my blood into him.

It feels so fucking amazing that I'm tossed right into another orgasm, pressing the back of his head to my flesh as I give him whatever he needs from me.

If only for now...

The next morning, I wake up with the weak sun streaming in through his blinds, one hell of a smile tugging my lips.

Ah, Luna. I haven't slept that well in *years*.

Waking up with an arm thrown over my waist? It's bliss, especially since it's connected to my gorgeous vampire.

He's still sleeping when I wake up. I take a few minutes to just drink in his beauty. He's absolutely stunning while at rest. He told me last night as he pulled me against him that his routine was to patrol all night—which I knew—and to get a few hours down when the sun was at its strongest—which I had suspected. I thought that meant that he was going to stay awake, but he murmured that he'd waited two hundred years to sleep with his beloved. Now that I was in his bed, he wasn't going to wait a single night more.

And though he seemed to enjoy himself, stroking me, tasting me, then *biting* me, when he told me that, I wondered if he meant that he wanted to finish the night with sex. Nope. When Aleks said sleep, he actually meant *sleep*. Sated by the two orgasms he gave me, I began to doze immediately. He could've done anything at all to me, and I would've let him.

Instead, with his rock-hard erection nestled between my ass cheeks, his arms wrapped around me, he spooned me until I fell asleep in the safety of his embrace.

He followed after me eventually, still sleeping when I pick up his arm, settling it down on a pillow after I slip out of the bed. My phone is in my purse. I'm not surprised that there's a missed call from Gem's phone number on the screen.

Before Aleks wakes up, I tap out a quick message,

asking if there is any way we could meet up to talk. With Walker's latest threat still so fresh, I hate the idea of leaving Muncie—and I have no idea how I'd get my overprotective vampire to let me go without him—but I don't want to risk Gem, either. She was name-dropped in her birth father's note, and I'm not so sure she understands just how bad the situation in Muncie is.

Plus, I've got a thing or two I want to discuss when it comes to Aleks. With that in mind, I mention that I won't be free until after ten pm, leaving her to make of that what she will.

It's early. Not even seven in the morning when I send the message. I don't expect her to answer right away, but she does, and I let out a sigh of relief when she tells me that she'll meet me at Charlie's after Aleks's patrol starts.

Yeah. Gem understood my message all right.

Tossing my phone back into my purse, I climb into bed again. I don't know what tonight will bring, but if I can pretend that Aleks really is mine for a few hours more, I'm going to take them greedily.

CHAPTER 13

Later that night, I'm sitting at the far end of the bar, nursing my ginger ale, when the door opens and I feel that familiar prickle against my back.

Alpha.

Her wolf's undeniable dominance hits me and my much more submissive wolf first, then the spicy cinnamon scent I know all too well; it overlays everything in the townhouse, and it still lingers in Aleks's apartment. I have to squelch the tiniest hint of jealousy that wells up inside of me, pulling my lips in a genuinely welcoming smile as I swivel on my stool.

I'm not the only one who's noticed her arrival. As the door swings closed behind Gemma, she's already waving at some of the patrons, offering greetings to others. Though she's slender and kind of short—she's a few inches shorter than me, at least—as she strides through the crowded floor of Charlie's, a path seems to clear for her like she's come kind of hulking wrestler heading for the ring.

Even the humans sense that there's something different about the pretty blonde. She pulled her long hair back in a high ponytail, the length of it swaying as she stalks purposely forward. Despite the February chill, she's wearing a short-sleeved t-shirt; it's black, like her jeans, and the dark color makes the gold-plated fang she wears pop. Shifters don't feel the cold the same way that vampires and humans do, so she seems perfectly comfortable in her spring wear—even as a few stray snowflakes cling to her pale hair.

Huh. It must be snowing again. It wasn't when I arrived at the bar, but I was so antsy and anxious that I showed up early. I came straight from work, purposely avoiding Aleks. By now, he's probably out on patrol. That gives me some time before I have to face him again.

I need advice. The only two people I even considered asking for it were Gem and Leigh. Leigh is happily mated, and Tamera is another vampire. Only knowing that she would inevitably tell Tamera—then Gretchen—about my confusion when it comes with being with *the* Aleksander Filan had me hesitating.

Gem is a shifter. True, her mate is another alpha, but she'd understand the mating dance much better than Leigh would. Plus, she knows Aleks extremely well, and meeting with her gave me an excuse to decline Gretchen's invite to join them at Mea Culpa tonight.

Then there's the undeniable fact that she also knows what it's like to be courted by him...

My grin wavers. Was this a bad idea? I really hope not.

Because here she is, and before I can think twice about this, she's plopping herself on the empty stool to my right. "Hey."

"Um. Hi. I—"

"Gem!"

Leaning back, looking down the length of the bar, she beams over at the pair of men waving at her. "Vin. Jimmy. Long time no see."

One of them is an older human. I'd put him at over sixty, with the grey hair and wrinkles bracketing his mouth and his eyes to prove it. He lifts his drink—a tentative sniff tells me it's whiskey—in Gem's direction.

The other man is a supe. Vampire. He looks like he's in his thirties, though his aura marks him as much older. He has slicked-back dark brown hair, pale grey eyes, and a lascivious smile as he greets Gem. A shot of chilled blood is set in front of him. Grabbing it from the countertop, he slips off of his stool, sidling down the bar until he's sitting on the other side of Gem.

"Off duty, Vin?"

"Nah," he says. "Just grabbing a drink before I head back out. What about you? If you're looking for Hailey, she's been out all week. Something about celebrating getting her fang and her man."

"I heard. Good for her. I wasn't sure Dominic would ever make it official, but I'm glad he did. Hailey deserves a Cadre vamp as her mate. But I'm not here for her." She bumps her shoulder against mine. "I'm meeting this one."

Easy touch is still difficult for me; with anyone except Aleks, that is. I tense as she hits me, bracing myself even as her carefree bump sends me listing a few inches to my left.

Gem might be small, but the alpha female packs a big punch.

As I re-seat myself, I focus on her mention of Dominic. If he's the same one I know—and I'm thinking so, since she called him a Cadre vamp—then Hailey must've been the female he wanted me to break his bond with Felicity for. Thinking back, I do remember him talking to her at the bar the night of my interview, but I never put two and two together until now.

Good for Dominic, then. He's been nothing but pleasant to me—gracious, too—and he's one of Aleks's friends. I'm glad he's happy with his new mate.

I just wish it could be that easy for Aleks and me...

The dark-haired vampire clears his throat. "Say, Gem. You gonna introduce us to your new friend?"

"Sure thing." She points at the vampire. "That's Vincent St. James. His buddy is Jimmy Fiorello"—she raises her voice—"who knows all about supes but is still sitting a couple of seats down like he thinks us shifters are gonna sniff his ass or something."

I nearly choke on Gem's obvious tease. It was so unexpected, especially when the older human jerks his chin in acknowledgement of her words. "That's got nothing to do with it. Was just finishing my drink, is all."

"Mm-hmm." Her eyes sparkle, and it's obvious that she misses them. "Anyway... guys, this is Elizabeth. She's like me."

"In more ways than one, I see," Vincent murmurs before taking a small sip of his blood.

What is that supposed to mean?

I don't know, and Gem ignores him as she adds, "She would've been behind the bar if Charlie didn't turn her down."

To my surprise, a bitter note finds its way to her tone. She wasn't happy when I told her that I didn't get the job, though she was mollified when I explained that I was working for Roman instead. It has all worked out in the end, but I guess she still harbors some annoyance that Charlie backed out of their deal.

I hadn't expected a reason why he didn't hire me.

He interviewed me, and he passed. It happens. But Gem... she felt like he owed her one and it still obviously bothers her that he didn't have one.

Seems like nobody told Vincent that, though, since he takes another sip before telling her, "Yeah. I heard about that. Bad luck. Filan really didn't want Charlie to hire another shifter. I think you broke his heart, Gem."

Her good cheer from earlier dims a little further, a flush rising high on her cheeks. "Oh, stuff it, Vin."

He gives her a wistful look. "I tried. You kept on telling me no."

Reaching out, she shoves him, the vampire chuckling to himself as he moves on the stool.

Once again, I can't help but think that it must be nice to be able to touch someone as easily as that...

I shouldn't be jealous. For so many reasons, I shouldn't be jealous of Gem—but I am. She's strong. Powerful. Dominant. Her wolf doesn't cower like mine does. She's a fierce fighter, and a protective female. She wears an Alpha's marks on her skin, but she's kind, too. She's been looking out for me ever since we met in the district, and even if she has history with Aleks, she doesn't use that against me one way or another. She's a sweetheart.

But, most of all, I'm jealous because I think she *did* break Aleks's heart.

She's not his beloved. Julia was once, and I'm supposed to be now. Gem was never his beloved—but he wanted to be bonded to her anyway. When she rejected him, taking Ryker for her mate instead, Aleks didn't handle it well.

And I know I never would've met him if it wasn't for her. Aleks only showed up at the Wolf District because Ryker asked him to look out for Gem. Does that do anything to soothe this new burst of jealousy?

Not even a little.

Once she's recovered, she narrows her golden eyes on the vampire. "Hang on. What do you mean, Aleks didn't want Charlie to hire her? What the hell does he have to do with Elizabeth working the bar?"

The vampire's easy laugh ends abruptly. With an "oh shit" expression on his face, he shifts in his seat, reaching for his glass of chilled blood. Vincent drinks some more as a distraction, grimacing when he sees that Gem has locked her unblinking alpha stare on him.

He gulps. "I take it you didn't know that he's the reason Charlie said no."

Gem glances my way. I shake my head.

Her eyes go from vivid to molten. "Nope."

Honestly, I should've guessed. Maybe not right away—I didn't know Aleks all that well when this started—but since then? Yeah... I should've guessed. With the sway he has in town, the only one who would dare go against him when it comes to his beloved is Roman Zakharov.

Poor Charlie never had a chance.

Gem's obviously thinking along the same lines as me. She must be, because she actually lets it go. Something tells me that she won't for long—poor Aleks should expect a text in the future, and probably Charlie, too—but she doesn't give either of them shit for it right now.

Instead, she turns to look at me. Behind her, I see Vincent's shoulders sag in relief before he tosses back the last of his shot. Murmuring a quick goodbye, he hightails it out of the bar.

When I see Gem's determined expression, I almost want to follow him.

"I can't be here long. Ryker's spent the whole evening holding a joint council with our pack and Kendall's. He's the—"

"Alpha of the River Run Pack," I supply absently.

What can I say? When you're a lone wolf, you keep up to date on pack politics.

Gem gives me a strange look but doesn't comment. "Yeah. Anyway, he'll have my hide when he finds out I came down here without telling him, especially this late, but you made it sound urgent so... here I am. What's up?"

My insides twist with guilt. "I don't want to get you in trouble with your mate," I begin.

She waves me off. "It's fine. I like it when he spanks me." Shooting me a grin when my mouth drops open, she lays her hand on my stool, giving it a subtle shake. "Come on. You told me about my sperm donor's note. Aleks just said that Roman would get in touch with Ryker. He'll give me details when he gets them, but he's busy with Kendall. I need to know what's going on. Tell me. What happened?"

Her wolf is still in control despite the fact that Gem is in her skin. And while it wasn't quite a command—at least, not a deliberate one—I can't help but react as if it was.

Tell her?

Okay.

I tell her *everything*. Starting with the unfamiliar shifter's scent leading up to the townhouse and the slaughtered vampire he left for me to find along with Walker's note, all the way to how I ended up staying over with Aleks last night, I don't stop until I get to the point when I decided to call her and ask her to meet with me.

But not about the Alpha's delusional idea that I'll end up as his mate. That's my problem, and after how she challenged him and won, I doubt Walker will try attacking the Mountainside Pack until he's leading a pack as powerful as the Western Pack once was.

No. There's something else I want to talk to her about. I'm just waiting for the right moment to bring it up.

The whole time I'm telling her about last night,

keeping my voice as low as possible so that I'm not overheard, Gem doesn't interrupt except to ask if I have a copy of Walker's note. Pausing only to send her a message with the picture I snapped of it before Aleks pocketed it for Roman, I continue talking while she nods, staring at the dark lines scrawled on the blood-stained paper.

"I'll have to let my mate know about this. No one's heard from Walker in months... Luna, we're still trying to figure out how he popped his head into town last week... but he's like a ghost. No one can find him. To have him do this? He's getting closer to making his next move."

And, unfortunately, it's against *me*.

"I know. And I would've told you last night. Only..."

"It's okay. I get it. I know how Aleks is, and his need to run everything through the Cadre. I'm actually surprised he's not here, acting in its interests as you tell me all about this."

"He's on patrol," I explain.

"Yup. Know all about his insane need to patrol at least eight hours each night, every night. I think he had like four nights off the whole time I lived with him. It won't be easy to get that workaholic to settle down."

I shrug.

I mean, who says I want to? Besides, I like that about him. It shows how protective of a male he is; he considers Muncie his territory and, like shifters, he's willing to do anything to protect it. But when I called him last night, in trouble and in need, he immediately ran to my side.

He protects me, too. Answering my call, coming when I'm in trouble, bringing me to his house... that's exactly how a bonded, possessive shifter acts.

Huh. Maybe it's not just a shifter thing, but a *supe* thing.

That's something to think about.

After sparing a glancing at the time flashing across her screen, Gem puts it back in her pocket. "You know... I've got a little more time if you need anything else from me."

"Oh. Um... I don't know."

"I mean it. Look, Ryker already had the whole pack looking for Walker before this, and a dead vamp is probably Roman's problem, but when it comes to Aleks... you want to talk to me about him some more?"

Do I? "Not really."

Gem laughs. "Appreciate the honesty."

Was that rude? It felt rude.

I sigh, then blurt out, "He moved me into his apartment. He *cooked* me *dinner*."

It's such a huge confession for me. But Gem? She's not even a little surprised by it.

She shrugs. "Made it longer than I did. I was living with Aleks within days. Took me months before I ate his food, though, and only because I made it clear we would take turns." A curious twist of her lips as she asks, "You in my old room?"

She'll know if I lie. It's an alpha thing. She'll *know*.

"I slept in his bed last night."

Her eyes light up. "Did the two of you mate?"

"Gem!"

"What? It's a valid question. He's your fated mate. You're his beloved. The Luna's almost full. I still told myself I hated Ryker the first time we mated, but that didn't stop us."

You're his beloved...

So she believes that, too?

And maybe it's a valid question to her, and she obviously has no problem talking about her sex life with her alpha mate, but I'm a little uncomfortable discussing what went on between Aleks and me—especially with half of Charlie's as an audience.

I don't have to, though. With the tiniest flaring of her nostrils, she knows exactly how far we went last night.

Ah, Luna. Now I'm bushing.

Gem notices. "Hey. You like him?"

Do I? Yes. More than I should. When it comes to *love*, I'm a little less certain, but *like*?

I nod.

Gem pats me on my shoulder. "Thought so. Okay. Can I give you some unsolicited advice?"

I don't think there's any way I can stop her. "Sure."

"Listen to your wolf. Sometimes our people brains get in the middle of a good thing. Screw the brain. When it comes to your forever, it's your gut and your heart you want to pay attention to. If your wolf wants him, take him."

"I don't know."

"I'm not telling you to bond yourself to him right now. You couldn't tonight even if you wanted to. But… would it really hurt to give him a test drive?"

Oh my Luna. I don't think anyone is really paying us any attention right now. Doesn't matter. I feel like I'm about to die from embarrassment.

And Gem's still not done.

"If your two-legged half is giving you hang-ups, rely on your wolf. Maybe you need to get in touch with your wild side." With a wink, Gem lowers her voice so that I'm for sure the only one who can hear it when she murmurs, "There's a park not too far from here that I recommend."

The sad thing is I know exactly which one she means since it's where I almost jumped Aleks the first time I gave him my blood.

I grab my glass. There's still a mouthful of flat soda at the bottom. I hurriedly drink it, trying to cover up my sputtering.

"What?" Gem's suddenly so innocent, I finally understand how she was able to pass as an omega wolf for most of her life. "Was it something I said?"

"It's just…" The glass clinks against the countertop as I set it down. On a sigh, I admit, "I don't even know if he likes me back."

It's like I'm a fifteen-year-old virgin again. Even in a shifter pack, we all have those awkward years where we worry about who likes who, who will be the first to fuck, and what our future bonded mates will be like.

Now I'm drawn to a vampire, I haven't had sex since Kyle, and my mate…

I still want him. There. If I can't admit it out loud, I can at least admit it to myself. Fate has a way of pulling two souls who match together. Maybe Aleks needs a shifter female with dark hair, and I need a complicated male.

He's never shied away from considering me his. Even in the beginning, he allowed that there was a tie between us. He wants me to be *his*.

But it's true. I still have no idea if he likes me. Not my looks—so eerily similar to his Julia's—or my kind of supe—*everyone knows Aleksander has a wolf fetish*, scoffed Gretchen—but *me*. Elizabeth Howell, a Luna-touched female who longs for her mate.

Gem cocks her head slightly. "Are you sure?" A devilish glint comes to her gaze as she adds, "Aleks hasn't done anything to make it obvious that he wants you? Not me, not some ghost of his past, but *you*?"

I think back. "He sent me a box of tea when I first got the job with Roman."

"Aleks does so love his tea. What else?"

"He also brought me my favorite sandwich for lunch."

Gem nods sagely. "Now that? That sounds like something a shifter would do to court his mate."

She's got a point.

He is a vampire, though. My instincts tell me to treat him like any other wolf during the mating dance, but while he's a supe, he's no shifter.

Hmm.

What about me? Aleks brought me food, *cooked* me food, when he doesn't need it. What can I do to reciprocate?

I fed him my blood twice now. The first time it had been an emergency. The second? I was so mindless with pleasure that I gave him permission without even realizing what I was doing.

There was an intimacy to the act that's undeniable, but a mating—despite the name—is more than just sex. It's caring for your partner. Protecting them. Taking care of them.

Feeding them...

Aleks eats human food out of habit, not necessity. I know he goes to donors like the rest of the vampires in Muncie, but his fridge is also full of bagged blood for when he feels like "eating in". If I brought him some back to the apartment, it'll be like him picking up a sandwich from the deli with me in mind.

Pursing my lips, I look up at Gem. "Do you think you can get Charlie to sell me one of his bags?"

She grins. "Yeah. I think so. Sit here. I'll be right back."

And then, visibly satisfied with herself, Gem disappears behind the bar.

CHAPTER 14

Ten minutes later—after Gem tracks down Charlie, then says her goodbyes to her old customers—I'm leaving the bar with a blonde shadow and a bag of chilled AB positive in my tote bag.

Even through the thick plastic and the canvas material, I can scent the rusty, tangy blood. You'd think it would bother me. When I first arrived in Muncie, it took me a few days to get used to the meaty, cold scent that clings to vampires, but blood? It often triggered my wolf's predatory instincts.

Not now. Not when I think of it as an early morning snack for Aleks.

Huh. Look at me. Getting all domestic over my new roommate.

As we step onto the street outside of Charlie's, I go

still. My wolf whines, eager to rub flanks with Gem's, hiding behind the alpha's dominance. Taking a deep breath, I filter out the smells from the bar—booze, food, and BO—and the blood in my bag until all I'm left with is a forest-scented musk that undoubtedly belongs to a wolf.

My head jerks to my left. There, on the corner, is a boyish-looking male with sandy brown hair and soft golden eyes. His thumbs are hooked in his belt loops, his shirtsleeves rolled up to his elbows, leaving his forearms on display. He was watching the entrance like a hawk, already moving toward us before the door swings closed behind our backs.

It's not snowing anymore, but the ground is covered with a dusting. There's a bitter chill on the breeze. He should be wearing a coat. Even if his eyes and his scent didn't give him away, his outfit did—as well as his direct pursuit.

It's another shifter. A delta.

Interesting.

"Are you ready, Alpha?" he says. His voice is pleasant and a touch smooth. It's nice.

"Yup," answers Gem. "I probably pushed my luck staying this long, but it was worth it. I've got a lot to tell Ryker. Was everything okay out here?"

"Everything's fine."

"No sign of another wolf?"

His eyes flicker over to me. "Just this one."

It's a quick up and down, up and down before he moves a little closer. The first up and down I can understand; this is obviously one of Gem's "guards", and he's checking me out to make sure I'm not a threat to the Alpha of the Mountainside Pack's mate. The second one, though? Yeah. He was just *checking me out*.

Gem gestures at me. "This is Elizabeth. Ryker knows her. She's safe."

"Silver eyes? That's unique." His lips quirk in a flirtatious smile. "Hi. I'm Bobby."

Gem cuts in front of me. Then, planting her hand against his firm chest, pushes him a few steps back. "And she's unavailable. Down boy." Turning toward me, catching my surprised expression, she rolls her honey gold eyes. "Come on. We both know you have Aleks's fang in your pocket. If he catches Bobby's scent on you, I might lose another one of my guards the hard way."

The male shifter immediately takes another couple of steps away from us as I gape over at Gem.

I... I didn't tell her I had Aleks's fang. And, sure, Roman's isn't hanging off my neck anymore, but that could just mean I removed it. Vampires can sense the mark of one of their kind. Another shifter shouldn't be able to, even if they *are* an alpha.

Instead of asking her how she knows—I think my new roommate is conspiring with his former roomie more than I thought—I just wonder, "Whose side are you on?"

She won't tell me Aleks's secrets, and she's obviously been giving him hints on how to court me the way a shifter would. At the same time, she has no problem telling me to listen to my wolf while also making sure I had some insight into the vampire by passing along that Polish to English dictionary.

Is she helping me or Aleks? Ryker warned her to let Fate play out when he picked his head up from his map and realized the extent of Gem's meddling that night, but would I be walking out of Charlie's with a bag of blood if it wasn't for her?

Her impish grin is proof that she knows exactly what she's doing. "Both?"

I close my eyes and shake my head.

Yeah. That sounds about right.

I'M HALFWAY BACK TO ALEKS'S APARTMENT BUILDING when the wind shifts and I suddenly go motionless.

I smell *wolf*.

Over the last few weeks, it seems I might've become nose-blind to all of the vampires that live in Muncie, but I haven't caught a hint of another shifter—excluding the unknown shifter who left Walker's mess for me to find—since I ran into a lone wolf during my last stint at that small town Christmas carnival. The female had lived a life similar to mine: pretending to be human, hiding out from our kind, while supporting herself any way she could. I closed up my table immediately, not wanting a pissing contest when she flared her golden eyes at me.

She had done a double-take when she noticed that my shifter eyes were silver, but that didn't stop her from unleashing her claws—or maybe that's why she did. Either way, I had to go.

But, somehow, my wolf has started to think of all of Muncie as hers, not just the townhouse. From the downtown area where Charlie's is, to Aleks's apartment, all the way to the center where Roman lords over the Cadre building... it's mine.

I'm the only wolf allowed inside of Muncie.

Walker's scent clung to the note that he left, but he wasn't the shifter who slaughtered Anton, leaving me for him to find. I still don't know who that was, but the scent that I pick up now?

I know this one.

Peyton.

She's not just lurking on the edge of Muncie's borders. She's found a way inside, and now she's taunting me.

Worse, she threatened to take Aleks from me. And, okay, I don't know exactly what's going on between us. My wolf won't let me forget that he's my fated mate—

neither will the Luna—and he seems determined to prove to me that I truly am his beloved.

But after last night? I feel closer to him than ever. With Gem's advice bouncing around my skull, I've finally started to think that there might just be a chance for me and him.

There won't be if Peyton decides to target him.

Aleks is out on patrol. If she's made it inside of Muncie, she could be going after my mate just like she swore she would. And with everything changing between me and Aleks so quickly, he has no idea that she threatened him—or that Peyton even exists.

Okay. Think, Elizabeth. What do I do now?

Gem's out. She's too far to ask for her or her guard's help. I could call her, but that would only waste time.

I can't tell Aleks now. Over dinner last night, I asked him where he was all those days where he seemed to have disappeared. Though I could tell that he didn't really want to let me know, he eventually confessed that he was expanding his patrol. Roman gave him the okay to go farther and further to keep Muncie safe. Anton's murder at the hands of a wolf had caught the head vampire's attention.

Aleks's, too. Only, he added in between nonchalant sips of his tea, he was determined to track down the Wicked Wolf wherever he could be. If he was gone, that was one less person who could come between the two of us.

He wanted to protect his beloved so that, this time, he got to keep her.

I didn't know what to say to that last night, and I'm just as speechless today. One thing for sure? If I called Aleks and told him I caught the scent of a shifter inside of Muncie, he'd drop whatever he was doing to go after her.

I'm almost positive that's what she wants, too.

Maybe I'm acting a little bit like a possessive, bonded shifter myself because, suddenly, I know exactly what to do.

Stop her.

Shoving past the humans walking along the sidewalk, I start with a quick-paced walk before turning it into a jog, then an outright sprint. Now that I have her scent and I'm on the pursuit, I won't let anything get in the way of me and my target.

I barely notice it when the sidewalk under my shoes becomes hard dirt. Just under Peyton's signature sweet scent, earthy notes hit me. Mud. Ice. Grass. Woods.

Park.

Even if we live in a city where we're surrounded by skyscrapers, automobiles, and way too many humans, shifters will always search out the wilderness. I did when I first arrived in Muncie; it became the place where I let my wolf run free. Looks like Peyton did, too.

And maybe it's a trap. Could be. I won't know until I track her down.

But now that I'm tucked among the trees?

I don't even bother kicking off my shoes. I just shift, letting my white wolf out as everything I was wearing—panties, socks, bra, shirt, jeans, and shoes—are obliterated with how badly she wanted to take over the hunt.

But whether I took a wrong turn or I got distracted during my shift, I'll never know. Peyton's scent fades as suddenly as I picked it up. I can't find her, but my need to protect my mate is too powerful to ignore.

I race through the woods, searching for... for something.

And that's when I hear Aleks.

"Elizabeth!"

I'm torn between two instincts: continuing to run after my prey, or responding to my mate. With my wolf out, it's almost impossible to deny the growing bond stretching between me and Aleks.

My wolf stops short. She wants her mate, and now that she recognizes his aura reaching toward her, she plops her haunches in the old layer of snow.

If I leave it up to her, she'll roll over onto her back, exposing her belly to Aleks, begging him to love her.

I need more control than that. And the only way to get that is to put my human side in charge.

So I do.

Seconds later, I hear his shoes crackle over the old snow. My head was already staring in the direction from which he was coming because I was able to pinpoint the source of the aura.

Of course, that means that when Aleks appears past the trees, he gets a dead-on look at my skin.

He goes immovably still for a heartbeat before he recovers. "You're naked."

Too late do I realize that I made a huge mistake.

Nudity isn't a big deal in a shifter pack. It's only when sexual need comes into play that it's obvious just how open—just how *vulnerable*—I am when I'm in my skin. And last night? We were intimate for the first time so sexual need is definitely there. And though I know his vampire sight is as impressive as my wolf's, that he saw everything I had to offer from below the waist, he tasted me under the cover of darkness.

With the Luna bathing my skin, every inch of me is on display.

"I had to shift to run," I tell him, purposely avoiding the part where I destroyed my clothes, lost my bag, and was chasing after a threat. His fang was in my pocket, and I only hope the magic that let Roman's transform with me means that I'll find Aleks's again in the future otherwise I'll have to tell him the truth about what happened.

But that's later.

Now? Now I have something else on my mind.

He rubs his mouth with his hand. Still staring at me unblinkingly, he murmurs, "You're not cold?"

I'm not. Shifters run hot, and the look Aleks is giving me? It's burning me up.

"No. You?"

He has on an expensive-looking sweater that's perfectly fitted and a pair of black pants. Perfect for an upscale dinner in October, a little overdressed style-wise—and underdressed weather-wise—for an evening patrol in the second week of February.

"I'm a vampire. I'm already dead, aren't I? Can't get any colder than that."

True. Though we both know that, with blood taken straight from the vein, he'll warm up pretty quickly.

I blink, a thought coming to me. And maybe it's because I've always gotten a little turned on during a hunt, and I hadn't been able to slake the need to protect Aleks by chasing down Peyton, but the more he watches me with that stunned stare, the more aroused I'm growing.

He looks like he likes what he sees.

I desperately want him to.

Not only that. With his eyes beginning to develop that tell-tale red rim around his pale irises, I realize that I want *him*.

I don't even have to look up to know that the Luna isn't at her most powerful yet. I could enjoy him without worrying about claiming him since the only way a shifter can claim their mate is through the Luna Ceremony.

I'd have to get the Luna's blessing—while she was full—then mate him, and mark him. He'd have to mark me back, and then I'd have to willingly keep it.

Even if I wanted to tie myself to Aleks officially, I can't tonight. But if he's willing to take what we have one step further…

I'm ready.

To be fair, I wanted to last night. I denied it beforehand, but in the heat of the moment, when Aleks sank his fangs in me, I almost begged for him to use his cock instead.

As Aleks stares at me, I drop my gaze to his crotch. My vision is keen enough that I can see the notable bulge pushing up against his tailored slacks.

My body is ready to mate. So is Aleks's.

But is he?

I'm not a brave female. I'm not dominant. I have a tendency to obey, and my default is to run before I willingly put myself in a dangerous situation. I have to be backed into a corner to fight. When I became Walker's prisoner and his pet? His threat to out me to the Alpha collective—who, he assured me, would put me down as an abomination to our kind because of my family's "gifts"—was enough to keep me in my place. Not even after Gem arrived in California, promising to help me escape, did I ever think it might be possible.

Years ago, though, before I became even more of a lone wolf to protect myself, the only time I showed any backbone was when it came to mating.

That's why I was so frustrated last night. The old Elizabeth, seventeen and carefree, would've told Aleks exactly what she wanted.

I'm twenty-nine. I've spent ten years on my own, and the one time I gave in to the urge to take a male, it ruined my life.

It won't be like that with him, the Luna tells me. *He's yours.*

He is—and it's time I take him.

I move into Aleks. My wolf is snapping her teeth at me, telling me to hurry up. The Luna goes silent now that she can sense what I'm about to do.

His eyes follow every move I make. Every sway of my hip. Every bounce of my tits. If I want to seduce my vampire, I have to make it worth it, and I put as much effort into it as I can until I'm standing right in front of him.

Then, before I lose my nerve, I reach out and cup him.

CHAPTER 15

He's so hard, I know I made the right choice. He needs relief, and I'm just the female to give it to him.

He shudders out my name. "Elizabeth…"

I loosen my hold on him, trading my palm for two fingers. I run them up and down his erection. "Is this okay?"

"It's more than okay."

"Good."

Aleks closes his eyes, throwing back his head as I add a little more pressure. I can't tell if he knows that he's doing it or not, but he begins to rock with the motion, showing me exactly where he wants to be touched.

I'm more than happy to oblige.

He lets me, though his eyes snap open again when my questing fingers find the button to his pants.

Reaching down, Aleks takes my hand in his. "I want you to," he says thickly, his accent suddenly more noticeable than it's ever been before, "but if you feel like you have to do this because of last night..."

That thought never crossed my mind.

Seduction, Elizabeth. Make him want this.

Make him want *you*.

I lower my fingers again, stroking him gently. "You're the one who said we don't reciprocate, right?"

He shifts his pelvis, giving me easier access to him. "I did."

"So why would you think that I'm doing this only because of the pleasure you gave me last night?"

Another stroke, higher up this time so I can reach for his zipper.

"I... I don't know."

Have I ever heard my vampire admit that? I don't think so, and if that doesn't make up my mind that we both need this, nothing will.

"I want you to know me, Aleks. The real me. Elizabeth. And Elizabeth can be very selfish when she wants to. I want you to feel good but"—I grab his zipper, tugging it gently down past the material of his boxers—"I want to feel even better. I ache. You have something that will make me feel better. Will you let me have it?"

I can only imagine what he's thinking. In the matter of a couple of days, I went from denying him, to seducing him out in the woods. But I mean every word I say, and he knows it.

Before I can reach inside of his boxers, searching for his cock, he lifts his hands, grabbing me by my arms.

"Elizabeth," he rasps out. "Look at me."

I do.

The only times I've ever seen Aleks looking so fierce were when he was about to fight for his life. And yet... I'm not afraid.

"Yes?"

"Are you my beloved?" he demands. "Do you accept me as yours?"

At this moment in time, when we're on the cusp of something great between us, I can.

"*Yes*."

Aleks shutters his eyes, the fierce expression traded for a wicked look full of the promise of pleasure—and sin.

Just then, I almost tell him that he's my fated mate. The words rise up into my throat, perching themselves on the tip of my tongue.

But... I don't.

It would only be a complication if this doesn't work out. Until I can be sure that our bond is secure, that Aleks accepts me for *me*, I don't think I can tell him.

He'll use Fate against me. If my blood assured him that I'm his vampire mate—which, well, obviously—and both my wolf and my goddess whisper the same when it comes to him, he won't stop until he's claimed me.

That's the thing. With my abilities... I've seen too many bad bondings. Mates who stayed together because they had to, not because they loved each other and couldn't imagine life without their partner.

Do I love Aleks? I... I don't know. At the very least, I'm halfway there, and it's definitely my human side that's hesitating.

Then again, it's also my human side that is dying to have some closeness with Aleks. A connection.

An intimacy.

I need him to want me, and when he shoves both his pants and his boxers down, freeing the most gorgeous cock I've ever seen in my life, I am undeniably convinced that he *does*.

Aleks kicks off his shoes, then hurriedly strips off his pants and his boxers. Then, with one practiced motion, he rips off his sweater so quickly that his muscles are still rippling before he drops it to the dirt.

He advances on me, the hunger in his eyes so stark, yet arousing. "You're mine. Forever."

I'm his.

For tonight.

Pulling my naked body into him, he hooks his arms under my bare thighs. Shifters are solid. I weigh a good one-sixty, easy, and he lifts me up as if I'm as light as a feather. He settles me just above his hips, encouraging me to wrap my legs around him as he digs his thumbs into my ass cheeks.

Using his strength, he bobs me up and down, spreading my wetness along his cock. It's already pointing skyward, ready to mate, but instead of him angling his hips to line our bodies up right, he teases me. My folds are slippery. As he bounces me easily, I rub against him, amazed at how strong my mate is— and how good his hard cock feels every time he bumps against my clit.

I'm achy. I feel so empty inside, but he seems to be enjoying himself, using my body as his plaything. For a few seconds, I wonder if he's planning on stroking himself off without ever getting inside of me. Which would be okay. The whole point of this is to make Aleks feel good—

Nope. I'm still a Luna-awful liar. I want Aleks to mate me more than I want my next breath and I whimper my need to him.

"I'm almost ready, księżyca," he says, and though he doesn't seem winded at all, his voice is hoarse. I realize then that it's taking all of Aleks's control not to just plunge inside of me.

I just don't know *why*.

"I need to feel you inside of me," I gasp out before pleading, "Make me feel as good as you did last night."

"That's my intention," he promises. "I know you're ready for me, but if I'm slick with your need, I won't hurt you as I take you. You were so tight last night... I never want to cause you pain."

That's right. In the middle of him tasting me last night, he slipped a finger inside of me. I might not be a virgin, but it has been seven years since I've been with a male. To make this mating as memorable as possible, he's doing a little foreplay while also reacting to my urgent need to skip most of it right now.

But I'm ready. I'm more than ready.

Bracing myself by clutching his shoulders with my claws, I try to take control. I appreciate his need to put me first, but I'm a shifter. I can take whatever he can give me.

And I want him *now*.

My claws cut right through his skin. Aleks's blood perfumes the air. I didn't mean to mark him, but I'd be lying if I said that the realization that I *did* doesn't drive me nearly mindless with lust.

I throw back my head and, though it comes out strangled because of my human-shaped vocal cords, I howl.

My marking his skin does something to Aleks, too. Gripping his cock by the base with one hand, he pushes my ass up with the other until he's able to position himself right at my entrance. I moan when I notice that the head of his cock is as chilled as his skin, but as he starts to push, it only feels *amazing.*

Slowly at first, he begins to feed me inch by inch while I'm panting at him to give me *more*. When he's halfway in, Aleks finally accepts that all I'm feeling is a mixture of pleasure and delicious fullness. I can take it and, with one last push, he gives it to me.

Aleks bottoms out inside of me. My skin sparks with electricity as I lift my hands up, shoving my fingers into his curls.

He doesn't need me to ride him. Pistoning his hips as he tightens his grip on my backside, Aleks begins to fuck me more savagely than any other male has ever before.

And I *love* it.

Another wolfish cry tears out of my throat. I'm not thinking about tomorrow. I'm not thinking about his past, or my future. Peyton is a distant memory, a problem I can deal with later.

Right now, it's just me and my vampire.

Arching my back as he thrusts in and out of me, I grab Aleks by his head, dragging his lips to my throat. I don't even realize I'm doing it until his cool lips brush against the side of my neck.

"If you want it," I tell him with more emotion than I should, "take it."

He doesn't hesitate. My skin pinches for a split second, lost in the pleasure of his touch, as he slides his fangs inside of me at the same time as he buries his cock all the way to the hilt again.

While he sucks, he keeps our groins pressed together. In this position, with me in his arms, every pull on my neck goes straight to my clit. By the time he's taken his fifth pull, my legs are shaking. At his sixth, I start to come around him.

He moans around my flesh, slowly dragging himself in and out again as he slows down on sucking my blood. He hasn't taken as much as he has before—it's nowhere near how much he needed after he got stabbed with the silver knife—but I'm already a little dazed.

Of course, that's probably because of the orgasm I just had.

I'm still pinned on his length as Aleks finally releases his fangs. Looking down at me, I see that his eyes are fully red but, for the first time, I understand it's not just because of bloodlust.

It's just straight-up lust.

Disentangling my fingers from his hair, I grab him by the shoulders again. I push up, then fall. Again. Up, then down. I start riding him because, though I already came once, he's still rock hard.

I need him to find his pleasure, too.

And that's when he lifts his hand. He's still holding my weight with his other—proving he's even stronger than I thought—but his right hand? He curves it around the nape of my neck, doing the same thing I just did to him.

He guides my head to the side of his neck.

"Bite me back, księżyca. Take my blood inside of you. Take *all* of me."

I'm not a vampire. The only time I ever drink blood is when my wolf is out and she goes hunting for prey.

But if this is what Aleks wants from me, I'll do it.

In my two-legged shape, my fangs are barely sharper than a regular human's. Tapping into my wolf, though, gives me the strength to bury them past all of the layers of skin until his tangy, meaty blood—warm after he took so much of mine—fills my mouth.

The second it does, Aleks releases my neck, splaying both of his hands against the small of my back. He bucks once, then twice, before he hisses right as he finally comes.

The cold doesn't bother me; if it did, I could always become a white wolf again, with a built-in fur coat. Coming down from mating with Aleks? I'm so incredibly hot, I'd probably melt the snow in a circle around me.

Tell that to my vampire lover. He's still inside of me, eager to keep the connection even though I'm sure he finished. After nuzzling my cheek, he leads us to the ground, sprawling out on the snow-trampled earth. He lays on his back so that he's the one lying in the snow, holding me against him as I'm on top of him.

I've never been more comfortable.

He presses a kiss to the top of my head. "Mm... księżyca. That was wonderful."

I'm glad he thought so. I thought he was pretty phenomenal himself.

Tracing an aimless pattern on his naked chest, I murmur, "I looked that up, you know."

"Oh?"

"You have no idea how many tries it took me to figure out how to spell it. I never even got close." And my Polish is laughable at best. Only when I finally tried mimicking Aleks's low accent into my translation app did I get a match that made any sense. "You call me 'moon', don't you?"

Fitting, I had thought. Because my only worth is my connection to the Luna.

He lifts his hand, running his thumb down the length of my cheek. "It's your eyes."

"Huh?"

"They gleam like silver, but they go dark, too. Full moon. New moon. It seemed like a perfect name for you."

Oh. That... that wasn't what I thought at all.

Then again, when it comes to Aleks, he usually surprises me in the best ways.

"I like it," I say at last. "Can't promise I'll ever be able to pronounce it right, but I like it."

"We'll have a lifetime for me to teach you Polish."

I should probably point out that the sex we just had wasn't a promise for anything past tonight. But he's so relaxed, and maybe I'm being selfish, but I like him this way. I don't want to take away his happiness when, odds are, it'll be short-lived regardless.

I know we can't stay out here much longer, even if I wouldn't mind. Any vampire who might want to investigate the wild sounds I made during mating would immediately turn around when they realized that Aleks was the one who brought out my wolf even while I was in my two-legged shape. Humans, though? Other wolves?

Peyton?

I don't want anyone to ruin this moment we have together. We might have forever, or only just this one night, but I want to treasure it for as long as it lasts.

So, though I know we can't stay here, I lay my head on Aleks's chest, amazed at how still he is except for those few rare breaths he takes.

Just a few more minutes, I tell myself. Then I'll get up and start to figure out what I'm going to do next. Peyton might be gone—I'm willing to bet she is—but that doesn't change the fact that she was here.

Or that I just had the best sex of my life with Aleksander in the middle of the woods, but now I'm naked and I'm really not supposed to walk around Muncie in my fur.

I get about ten peaceful minutes before I hear the buzz of a phone vibrating. It can't be mine. Unfortunately, I lost mine somewhere near the entrance of the woods when I dropped my purse right before I shifted.

Which means it must be Aleks's.

His discarded pants are within arms-length reach of him. Tugging them closer to him, he plucks his phone out of his pocket, lifting it to his eyes so that he can read the message.

The lazy, easy mood evaporates in a heartbeat. With a sigh, he sits up, using his arm against my back to ease me to a sitting position with him. His jaw tight, he reaches out, snagging his sweater next.

"Aleks?"

"It's Roman. He needs us to come to headquarters."

Damn it.

And, really, I shouldn't be surprised. From everything I learned about him, Aleks is a high-ranking member of the Cadre. He's like Roman's Beta, his second-in-command. Not only that, but he's supposed to be on patrol. I distracted him.

I just hope that Roman doesn't want him to check on reports of some kind of wild animal crying in the middle of the park or something.

Hang on—

"Did you say 'we'?"

"That's what the message says. That he needs to see me, and that I should bring you along since he wants to talk to you and we're already together."

There goes my hope that Roman expected Aleks to pick me up and bring me to the Cadre's headquarters with him. I have no clue how, but my boss knows that I'm with Aleks right now.

When I ask Aleks how, he just shrugs and says, "Roman knows everything."

That's about right. In a shifter pack, the Alpha knows everything that's going on, too.

Which means he probably has an inkling that we just mated in the middle of the woods.

Oh, I'm not looking forward to facing my boss right now at all.

Too bad I don't have a choice.

CHAPTER 16

We make a quick pit stop at the apartment before heading to meet Roman. It tacks on a few minutes to our journey, but even Aleks agrees it's essential.

I have no idea what the head vampire wants with me. Unlike Aleks, I'm off duty, so it must be important otherwise it could've waited until morning.

I'm not about to meet my boss wearing only Aleks's sweater, though. And we'll only be later if I have to stop and claw out the eyes of every person—supe and human—who gives him an appreciative once-over as he walks the streets of Muncie with his sculpted chest out for everyone to see.

Good thing that the park isn't that far from his apartment. His area of the downtown is heavily vampire, so they obviously know what we've been doing by scent alone. Our half-dressed state—not to mention the clumps of snow clinging to my hair—is just a big honking clue that we got frisky outdoors. One good thing about Aleks's reputation as a high-ranking vampire in a Fang City? No one will dare say a word to him about it.

Now, I could've shifted back to my fur, but as much as it bothers me to have others staring at Aleks, he preens knowing that I'm wearing his bite and his sweater and nothing else. He pulled his silk boxers and his slacks back on after tugging the sweater on over my head; luckily, it falls just past my butt, so most of my goods are covered. He offered me his boots, but I turned him down. I'm a shifter. I'm used to walking around barefoot.

Walking around without panties? Not so much.

Aleks keeps his arm looped around my shoulder, tucking me into his side. Even after we go inside, each of us putting on a new change of clothes more fitting to meet Roman in, he takes my hand as we head back out again. Since mating, it's like he can't stand to have a few seconds when we're not touching in some way.

And, surprisingly, I'm perfectly okay with that.

I don't think I really understood how touch-starved I was until Aleks. Doesn't matter that I've developed iron-clad control over my abilities. That I have to willingly attempt to break a bond for it to work. Old habits die hard and I spent more than a decade guarding every caress.

With my vampire, I want all of them.

At this hour, Destiny is sitting where I usually am. Cameron is sitting beside her, leaning back in Leigh's chair. Though our usual relationship consists of a quick hello/goodbye as our shifts overlap, both of them shoot Aleks and me wicked grins as we enter the lobby.

We might've changed our clothes, but the scent of sex lingers on our skin. Plus, when Aleks got changed, I noticed that his new sweater is cut low—which, wouldn't you know, leaves my messy, frantic bite mark on full display. Given his vampire healing abilities, it'll be gone in a few hours, but it's still there and my colleagues know exactly how a powerful vampire like Aleks got them.

Don't blush, Elizabeth. Blushing around a bunch of vampires is never a good idea, but I'm a fully mature female. I can have sex for the sake of pleasure. It doesn't mean anything.

And, if I keep telling myself that, maybe I might actually believe it.

I HAD HOPED THAT ROMAN WAS TOO NOBLE TO SAY anything to us. Reminding Aleks that Roman is also my boss, I took my hand back right before we entered his office.

I shouldn't have bothered.

Roman looks up from his desk, running his gaze over the two of us. With the smallest curve of his lips, he mutters, "Finally. My congratulations to the both of you."

Next to me, Aleks puffs his shoulders out in undeniable pride. "Thank you."

"You've been a loyal friend, Aleksander. As good as my brother. For two centuries, I had to watch you mourn your beloved. I'm so glad to see that you found her again."

I stiffen. Right. Because even the lead vampire of the Cadre looks at me and sees another female's face.

"You lost yours, too, Roman. In the same war that stole my Julia."

Oof. That hurts. Aleks calling Julia his... yeah. That one hurt a lot.

I work hard to pretend like it didn't, instead focusing on what Aleks just said. I knew that Julia was one of the first casualties of the last decades-long Claws and Fangs war between shifters and vampires. But Roman lost his mate then, too?

I didn't know.

"The difference is that I had Kira for the six centuries before it. We both knew what we were risking when we went to war. Death can be inevitable at times, even for one as deathless as we. But your Julia didn't deserve her end, just like you didn't deserve to lose her before you'd ever bonded her to you."

I... I didn't know that, either, and something tells me that Roman only added that last part out loud for my benefit. They were never bonded? I guess I just assumed that Aleks was chasing another female to take over his broken bond, but I never doubted that he'd claimed her before she died.

Aleks doesn't deny it. His shoulders go tight, an unreadable look flashing across his face, but he doesn't deny it.

Roman rises up from his desk. "Don't make the same mistake with Elizabeth," he says, every inch the command. "She's yours now. Protect her."

"Roman?"

"I kept her safe for you while you were being ridiculously noble and staying away. That all changed when you tore my fang from her throat, throwing it on my desk. I'm just glad you finally found your way to each other at last."

"You did that?" I murmur.

"Not my proudest moment," Aleks murmurs back. Then, to Roman, he says, "You planned this?"

"Me? No. Fate did. I just..." He purses his lips for a moment, the tips of his fangs peeking beneath his thin upper lips. "I just helped her along a bit."

"I... I don't know what to say."

Me, neither.

"Then say nothing." He turns his back on us, stalking toward the window. "I called you to headquarters to talk of other things."

"Yes."

He doesn't say anything in answer to Aleks, though. At least, not right away. And when he does? It's the last thing I expected to hear.

"War is coming." His hands folded behind his back, Roman looks out his window, casting his pale gaze over the Fang City.

"We'll increase patrols," Aleks answers immediately.

Roman glances over his shoulder. "Da. We must." A shadowed expression falls over his face as he turns away again. "I never thought I'd live to see it break out again. After Marcel…"

"None of us blame you for that. He wasn't fit to lead the Cadre."

"And I am?" Roman chuckles softly under his breath, trying to smooth over his last comment. "Ah. Forgive me. I've grown maudlin in my old age."

"You're only nine hundred, Roman."

"True. And you've little more than two centuries. So young compared to me. And you've been without your beloved nearly as long. I'm glad your wait is over." Under his breath, he mutters, "Mine is, too."

Aleks's normally flawless features crease as his brow furrows. "Roman?"

The head vampire shakes his head. "It's nothing. Just thinking." Clearing his throat, he moves away from the window. "As for Elizabeth… Dominic has asked for a short leave to honeymoon with his beloved. I'd like to reward Tamera by approving her request to make Leigh a temporary sunset spotter with her. When you leave, I'll have no one to sit in the lobby during the day, keeping out those I don't want to see. And you know how much I hate to be bothered most of the time."

It's a small tease, a tiny attempt at humor. Only…

"Who says I'm leaving?"

He turns, glancing at Aleks.

Aleks presses his lips together so tightly, there isn't a hint of his fangs peeking through.

Ah.

Who said that? I think I know.

"For as long as I'm welcome here, Muncie is my home," I say simply. "And this is my job. I don't plan on leaving anytime soon."

Roman bows his head. "Very well. You heard the lady, Aleksander."

He did. But he's not happy about it.

When Aleks opens his mouth, Roman cuts him off with a regal wave of his hand. "Now that that's settled, on to other things. Aleksander? I have a task for you."

Aleks swallows back his earlier retort. "Of course, Roman."

"There's been a report of a breach near the back side of our borders." Back side... by the mountains of Accalia? "It was called in by one of our people. None of my patrollers have seen anything out of the ordinary, but they're not the best. You are. Check on this for me?"

"I... yes. Right away."

This time, when Roman nods, he's almost distracted. Turning away from us, he braces his forearm against the window, staring out over Muncie again.

I glance up at Aleks. He's watching his leader with a curious look, though he shrugs it off when he realizes that *I'm* watching *him*. With a small smile and his head tilted toward the door, I understand.

We've been dismissed.

I don't know if it's because of our meeting with Roman or not, but the atmosphere in Muncie seems so much more foreboding as we leave the headquarters together.

Neither one of us says anything until we reach the corner and I slip my hand out of Aleks's. He had taken it after we walked out of Roman's office, rubbing circles against my palm with his thumb as we took the elevator down together. I never told him that the enclosed space makes my wolf antsy—it's a shifter thing—but I didn't have to. Once again, I'm reminded how much history he has with other shifter females because he immediately tries to soothe my wolf the second the doors closed behind us.

In the lobby, I purposely glanced away from Cameron and Destiny's curious looks. Aleks offered goodbyes on both of our behalf, then went silent.

Until I break contact with him, that is.

"Elizabeth? Where are you going?"

"Home. You're the patroller, Aleks. Not me. I'm just a secretary."

We both know I'm more than that but, smartly, he doesn't point that out.

Instead, a muscle ticking in his cheek, he asks, "Home? Do you mean mine? Or Gem's townhouse?"

It takes some effort to ignore the pang I feel when he reminds me that my choices are Gem's place or his. "I was going to go back to your apartment, but the townhouse is fine, too. Didn't you say you got someone to clean up the mess?"

"Tak. Of course. But you're still welcome to stay with me." Brushing the backs of my fingers with his, he murmurs, "I'd prefer it."

The jagged edges inside of me smooth over just a bit. "Okay. Then I'll go there."

"I'll escort you back."

No time. If Roman got a report that there was a breach, Aleks can't just worry about me. As a patroller, it's his duty to watch out for every soul who lives inside of the Fang City.

"Focus on securing the borders first. I'll be fine. Don't worry about me, Aleks."

That was probably the worst thing I could've said to him.

"I must. You are my beloved. You will always come first for me. Tonight only made that more clear."

He says it so simply. So matter-of-factly. Like I should know that already.

I wish I did.

Reaching out, Aleks snags my hand again. My wolf chuffs at me when I immediately yank it back.

"Elizabeth..."

"Don't *Elizabeth* me. Please." I can't say it was just sex, because it wasn't. Still, we didn't finalize a bond tonight... so why is he acting like we did? Like he's already my forever mate when I was only—as Gem suggested—"trying him out for a ride"? "Maybe this is my fault. I should've asked this before... but what are you expecting from me?"

"That's simple enough. Forever."

"Aleks—"

"You asked me, księżyca. I answered." That's true. I did. "But I know you're still so young." Young? I'm pushing thirty! And, okay, Aleks has two centuries on me, but he's a vampire. To one of his kind, he's probably considered younger than I am! "I can wait a little longer for my forever. What's a year or two after two hundred?"

Oh, Luna. Two hundred years ago—when Julia died, and Aleks started the search for a chosen mate. He never found one until Gem, but he couldn't have her.

And now he wants me.

He says he'll wait. I'm not so sure he will.

Just in case, I say tentatively, "What about now? What do you expect for *now*?"

"You're my beloved. My mate. And I want everyone to know it."

That's the thing, though. I'm not. At least, not his *mate* mate. While there's no denying the sex we had, I didn't claim him as mine. Our bond isn't finalized. It *can't* be. Sure, I marked him with my teeth when I bit him, but the Luna isn't full. No full moon, no Luna Ceremony.

But wait— how does a vampire bond his beloved to him? I never asked, because I didn't want to be tempted, but after last night, then the park... maybe I should have.

No. *No.* With my ability, I'd know if he cemented the bond on his side. It's just the same as before, a fated tie that is strong, yet not quite unbreakable yet.

"How?"

Aleks dips his hand into his pocket. When he pulls it out again, the Luna reflects off of something hanging from his fist.

It's a golden chain. Even before he unfolds his fingers, I know exactly what is going to be laying against his palm.

"I had this made for you early this morning." The morning after we were first intimate. Of course. "I was going to give it to you when I saw you next, but then—"

But then, the next time we met, I basically seduced him before he had the chance.

I know it's not the first fang he pushed on me. That sucker is in my pocket.

"Show me your mouth."

He does. It's the opposite fang from the one he gave me the night we were at Mea Culpa. That one's fully grown back in, but his left fang? It's missing.

And I have no idea how I didn't notice that until now. I guess I've been a little distracted, but *still*.

Even though I carry his fang with me, that's not enough for Aleks. He couldn't just ask me for the one he already gave me, either. Of course not. He snapped off another, turning it into a necklace, and now expects me to just put it on.

I... this is all happening too fast. It was one thing to sleep with him under the Luna; he's my mate, and I couldn't resist the way he looked at me. Staying over at his apartment? It just makes sense since the townhouse has been compromised. Keeping his fang in my pocket... in Muncie, with the target on my back, I need the protection.

But to wear it around my throat? I wore Roman's because it made me untouchable. I'm not his mate, but he claimed me as his own to keep my abilities close as much to keep me safe for Aleks's sake. I have no illusions about that; besides, I was perfectly okay with the situation. If Roman was going to use me, I was going to do the same. Add that to the hefty paycheck he gave me and the sense of belonging I got by working with the Cadre and I definitely made out.

Aleks is offering me his protection, but that's not all. I've been living among vampires long enough to know what a necklace like that really means. Add that to how insistent he was on hearing me say that I believed I was beloved before we had sex and it's pretty freaking obvious.

If I put it on, I'm telling the whole supe world that I'm Aleksander Filan's intended mate. The bond might not be finalized just yet—on my side, we'd need the full moon, and I still refuse to ask how vampires complete theirs—but wearing his fang close to my heart? It's as good as saying that we will as soon as we get the chance.

I've known of Aleks for more than five months, but this... this *thing* we have going on between us? It hasn't even been a week and a half yet since he called me his beloved for the first time. And, sure, I grew up in a shifter pack where the Luna is revered, and Fate is our religion. Unclaimed matings like Jack Walker and his Janelle are an anomaly. When a shifter finds their fated mate, there usually isn't any hesitation. We trust that the Luna has picked the right mate for us.

And my goddess? She gave me a mysterious, sexy, possessive yet oh so caring vampire who looks at me and sees his past.

How can we have a future if I'm not sure whether he wants me for me, or because I'm his lost love's twin?

That's the problem right there. I've had to fight the pull toward Aleks ever since that night I caught him watching me outside of Walker's cabin. Then I spent months—*months*—traveling the country, doing everything I could to avoid him, before I inevitably ended up in Muncie.

I'm tired of running. I'm tired of my abilities being used against me.

Most of all, I'm tired of denying how I feel for Aleks.

Too bad jealousy and self-doubt are a bitch to shake. I want him, but if I ever heard him call me Julia again? If he looked in my silver eyes and he wished they were gold instead? Gem is his good friend, but he never called her his beloved. Would he give me his fang, but still carry Julia's portrait around in his pocket?

Would I always be a replacement?

If so, that would break me.

I want him, but until I can be a hundred percent sure that he wants *me* back, I really have to turn him down. No matter how proud I would be to wear Aleks's fang, to claim him as my intended in return... I don't think I can.

"Aleks—"

Intuitive as ever, he knows. Clenching the length of chain in his fist, hiding his fang, his pale green eyes seem to flash. "Is it because of what I am?"

What? He doesn't honestly think that I would reject him because of what kind of supe he is?

One glimpse at his face and I realize: yes, yes he does.

"No. Of course not."

Honestly, I've never minded the fact that he's a vampire. Because of what *I* am, I didn't have the luxury of developing a deep-seated prejudice like other shifters. I've had to blend in with humans, make allies of other supes. Julia herself proves it's not *that* uncommon for our races to mix. I mean, I tried bringing him blood back to the apartment!

"Then why? You feel something for me. I know you do. And you *are* my beloved. I've taken your blood. I've taken your body. You're mine, Elizabeth. I want everyone to know it."

I lower my eyes to the dirt. Seeing the emotion splayed across his beautiful face... I can't right now.

"If it's not because I'm a vampire, and you don't deny your feelings for me, then what is it? You've denied us before. I've shown you I can be a good mate to you. Why deny us again?"

"I—"

He cups my chin with his hand. With a gentle tilt, he forces me to look at him. "Księżyca? What is it?"

"I... I want to." I *do*. "But what if—"

"There is no *what-if*," Aleks says decisively. "There is me and you—"

"And Julia," I mutter.

With a sigh, he pulls away from me. "Will she always be a ghost between us?"

"I don't know." It's an honest answer. "We've only known each other for such a short while, Aleks. And I care for you." I'm pretty much head over heels for him. "But I just..."

"What? Tell me."

"I just can't be sure that, when you look at me, you see me instead of her."

There. I said it. My biggest fear, and one of the reasons why I'm keeping some distance between us.

Not for much longer, though.

This time, when he swoops back in toward me, he

braces my cheeks with both of his hands. He's trembling just enough for it to be noticeable, the chain nestled against his palm pressed against my skin as he keeps my head steady.

"I see you. Elizabeth Howell. Mój księżyca." Laying his forehead against mine, sharing breaths, he murmurs, "My beloved moon."

My heart rate kicks up. My pulse is pounding, blood thudding through my veins. It has to be a siren's call to my vampire. He doesn't respond to it, though. Gliding his hands from my cheeks down the hollow of my throat, his thumbs touching, he rests his fingers against my pulse points before slanting his mouth over mine.

I fall into his arms. Wrapping mine around his waist, for the moment at least, I let myself believe that I'm really his.

And a moment is all we get.

Out of nowhere, a fierce howl splits the air. It echoes, reverberating through the quiet night.

Aleks immediately pulls back, already in hunting mode. I'm not too far behind. Letting my wolf rise up inside of me, I push away from him, following the fading echo.

"That way." I don't quite recognize whose howl that is—and, if I do, I push down my suspicions—but I can tell where it came from.

He gives a jerking nod. "Yes." After stealing one

more quick kiss, he squeezes my shoulder and starts to tear off in the direction I pointed in.

I'm right behind him.

I haven't taken five strides before he whirls on me, cupping my elbows "Elizabeth? What are you doing?"

Isn't it obvious? "I'm coming with you."

He'd shoved the chain into his pocket before he took off. Almost as if by magic, it's back in his hand.

"Only if you put the fang on."

Really? "Aleks—"

"It's stronger when it's near the heart. Take it off after if that's what you want, but please. Wear it for me."

I can tell what he *isn't* saying. The wolf could be part of the Mountainside Pack—or it could be one of our enemies.

How can I refuse?

Looping the fang around my neck, I fasten it as quickly as I can. My wolf is already up, head cocked, growling softly under her breath as she pads around inside of me. Her fur is bristling but, to my amazement, she seems to settle down slightly the moment his fang lands between my boobs.

"Good?"

Aleks nods. "Let's go."

CHAPTER 17

I haven't left Muncie since the night I visited Gem and her mate in Accalia. After how Peyton ambushed me, I decided to rely on the strength of Roman's reputation to keep me safe in the Fang City. Without a fang of her own, I didn't think she would ever dare cross the border into Muncie.

I still don't know if she did earlier today. No denying I caught traces of her on the wintry breeze. She was near enough for her innate scent to carry to me, but considering I didn't find any footprints—or even paw prints—as I chased after it, I have no proof. And then Aleks found me and... yeah. It wasn't the first time sex made me forget all about the idea of Peyton.

When Roman sent Aleks to check up on the breach, I wondered if it would be the wolf I sensed earlier; when I heard the howl, I was sure of it, and I couldn't just go home. I had to go with Aleks. All patrollers go on foot so I had a couple of miles' jog to worry if I'm going to find a familiar shifter at the end of this hunt.

Would it be Peyton? What about the Wicked Wolf? It's been barely more than twenty-four hours since he made the move on the townhouse Gem lent me, but even she's frustrated by the way he seems to have gone ghost for the months preceding his sudden reappearance. It doesn't matter that I'm not covering the Alpha's scent for him anymore. He can still hide which makes him infinitely more dangerous because none of us know *how* he is.

Then there's the fact that, to get inside the borders without it being considered a breach, he has to have a fang of his own to get in without being reported—and there hasn't been a report of another breach until tonight. Working for Roman, being the only shifter allowed to live in Muncie currently, I would've known.

During my first few weeks in the city, I'd already heard whispers of some kind of an uprising. While most vampires are content with Roman as their leader, not everyone likes his style. Some of the fanged supes have no problem working with shifters to get what they want.

And they want Roman dead.

I learned that when those two vampires—Hector and Anton—went after me. They wanted to hurt

Roman, and they threw Aleks's loyalty to him in his face before my vampire defeated both of them.

Any one of those "rebels" would snap a fang, hand it off to a shifter, then sit back and watch as they made Roman's difficult.

Like now.

I hope that this is all that is. That this is an easily thwarted attack on Muncie—on Roman—and not my past coming to bite me in the furry ass.

I manage to cling to that hope until we're about six blocks out from the edge of Muncie. When two well-known shifter scents—one sickly sweet like maple syrup, the other dark and bitter like burnt coffee—slam into me, I stumble.

Aleks is a few steps ahead of me. He's been leading the way, taking us on the quickest path with the least human obstacles. I thought he was entirely focused on the run. Should've known better. The second I stutter-step, he whirls around, grabbing my elbow so that I don't face-plant.

"Thanks." It comes out as a gasp.

"Are you alright?" Concern has red ringing his pale eyes. "What did you sense? The wolf?"

"Yeah. Two shifters." I hesitate for a heartbeat, before admitting, "The Wicked Wolf is one of them."

More of his irises begin to bleed red. Though he's careful no to mention his time in the district, Aleks has wanted to get revenge on Walker for how he made him his captive. Then the Alpha desecrated my sanctuary and only reinforced my vampire's hatred.

Did Roman know? When he got the report that there was a breach... did he know that it was Jack Walker out there? After our conversation earlier, I'm absolutely convinced that Roman treats life like a chessboard. He plans out every move ahead of time; the rest of us pawns just do what he expects. Like how he basically manipulated Aleks into treating me as his beloved. I can't blame him since I got a good job and a sweet wage out of it—not to mention Aleks's attention —but his sending Aleks to face off against Walker is just the sort of move I'd expect from Roman Zakharov.

"Any way I can get you to go back to the apartment while I take care of this?"

No, because that sickly sweet maple scent is equally recognizable. Peyton Slate is the other shifter waiting.

I shake my head.

Aleks huffs out one of his unnecessary breaths. "Thought so. Just—"

"I know, I know. Stay behind you."

"Ah, księżyca. You know me so well."

"Come on." I press my hand to the middle of his back, pushing just enough to get him to move. "We can't let them howl again."

I'm supposed to be the only shifter in Muncie. To be allowed to stay here, I had to keep that under wraps.

No shifting where a human could see me, and definitely no howling. The Fang City might back up against a mountain, but there shouldn't be any real wolves so close to the urban center.

Supes are an open secret here, but we're still a secret. And one of the two wolves is willing to jeopardize that just to act as a lure.

No way they knew Aleks would be the one sent after them. We were too far from the border when the howl sounded for them to pick up our scent, but when the second howl—richer, deeper, *angrier*—rips through the night, I know they're guiding us right to them.

Damn it. A second howl. Are they impatient or...

Ah. Definitely impatient and eager to brawl. From the dark edge of his wolf's power, I can tell that the Alpha came here tonight for a reason, and he's not backing down until he gets what he wants.

My wolf is torn. She wants to run to safety, but she also can't leave Aleks.

She's right. For good or for bad, he's our mate. We won't abandon him to the mercy of the Wicked Wolf.

Jack Walker is standing a few feet past the unmarked border that separates Muncie from Accalia; predictably, he's on the Muncie side. His legs are braced against the slippery snow, arms folded over his brawny chest. Damn if he isn't as handsome as I remember, with his styled blond hair and honey gold eyes.

Bastard.

It would've been so much easier to get away from him if his outsides matched his black heart and rotten nature. By the time I realized he was twisted and evil, I was trapped in the district. I never wanted to see him again.

And there he is.

He's not the only one, either. Her scent is even more cloying this close, or maybe that's the lovesick, puppy-dog look on her face as she stands a couple of steps behind Walker, staring at his profile.

Peyton.

My claws unleash at the sight of her.

She's staring at Walker, but he only has eyes for me as I come to a sudden stop. Once Aleks realized I had, he falters, falling back to stand beside me.

The Alpha sniffs, gingerly at first, then more noticeably. His nostrils flare, a black look crossing his face as he pinpoints what's different about me. Now that he has a nose full of Aleks's scent, he can tell that it's covering my skin.

He has to know that we mated. Oh, boy. Considering he has this crazy idea that I would ever choose him after rejecting his proposals for two years straight, that can't be good.

Surprisingly, Walker goes no to ignore the vampire

completely. I have no doubt in my mind that he is cataloging every tiny movement Aleks makes, but he acts as if he doesn't even notice he's there.

Good. The last thing I want is Walker paying any real attention to him.

"Ah. Elizabeth. I was beginning to think that if I had to wait for the parasites to roll out the welcome mat much longer, I'd just use this and take a stroll on inside."

Walker hooks his finger under the simple gold chain he has on, showing off the fang hanging there.

Well, that explains it. Just like I was afraid of, a Muncie vampire has betrayed the Cadre, working with their ancient enemy instead. Because, make no mistake, the Alpha isn't here to ally with Roman. If I know him as well as I think I do, he's here to take him down.

From the blast of chilled air coming off of him, my vampire's thinking the same thing.

"What..." It's a whisper. Only when Peyton tosses her hair over her shoulder, her expression as vicious as always when she's looking at me, do I find my voice. I'm scared of Walker, but not *her*. "What are you doing here?"

"I just told you. It's been nearly half a year and Luna knows I'm fucking tired of waiting. I've come here for two things. My loyal Beta is taking care of one." Beta? He still has one? "But for this..." Walker reaches down, not even discreetly adjusting himself. "I'll be taking my mate now."

My lips part as I gape in ill-disguised horror.

He can't mean me, right? Grabbing his erection, basically fucking me with his gaze while Peyton stands right behind him, Aleks at my side? Right?

Wrong.

Letting go of the fang, he crooks his finger at me. "Now, Elizabeth."

"What?" screeches Peyton. "But Jack... you told me *I* was going to be your mate."

Wait a second... was that what Peyton meant when she confronted me that first night? When she said she was going to take my mate?

She meant *Walker*?

If so, she was way off base. She can have the Wicked Wolf if she wants him.

Just leave Aleks alone.

Walker's gaze slides to his right, a sneer twisting his face. "You? You were good for a couple of fucks. Desperate times call for desperate measures and all that. But my mate? Oh, no, no, no. If I can't have Janelle, I want Elizabeth. No more fucking around." The sneer turns cruel as he looks back at me. "Did you enjoy my mating present?"

Oh, Luna... a vampire head in my bed was his idea of a mating present?

I gulp, staying silent.

He holds out his hand to me.

"Come over here, Elizabeth. You won't like what I'll do if you don't."

He means it, too. A sadistic bastard with countless challenges under his belt, there are so many ways he can hurt me.

And not just me.

Yup. Definitely still terrified of him.

My wolf rolls over to expose her belly as I take a hesitant step toward Walker. Before my foot can hit the snow again, Aleks lashes out, gripping me gently, keeping me at his side.

"Stay with me, księżyca."

"Elizabeth! Who is this vampire to tell you what to do?"

How many times did the Alpha use that same commanding tone with me? And how many times was I able to ignore it? Too many, and never—but that was before Aleks.

He answers so I don't have to.

"You don't recognize me, wolf?"

"Ah." Walker's lips curl. "It took me a second. You don't look the same without the silver bullets plugging up your chest."

"You dare come here again? After what you did to me? After what you did to Elizabeth? And you think she'll choose you when she could have—"

Aleks stops short before he can say the last word: *me*.

He doesn't have to. Walker's not stupid. He knows exactly what Aleks was about to say—just like he knows how to tuck that knowledge inside and use it at the opportune moment.

"What do I have to lose?" Beneath the moonlight, his honey gold eyes gleam. "Because of you"—he flings his left arm behind him, gesturing at the towering mountain at his back— "because of them, I have nothing. Can you blame me for trying to at least choose a mate?"

Peyton hisses.

Without looking behind him, Walker backhands her with his right arm, sending her flying to the snow-covered ground.

I guess she already had her one warning. She hits the earth hard, her hand flying to her face, but she doesn't question Walker again.

"My pack is gone. My territory is being divided up by scavengers. I have nothing," he repeats, "but if you won't give me my mate, I will have my war."

No.

Aleks hunches his body, lowering himself in an offensive crouch. "I won't be responsible for another one."

There's so much emotion in his declaration, I shiver. What... what does that mean?

I don't know, and if Walker does, he refuses to remark on it. Instead, with his jaw tight and his expression stubborn, he says, "I will."

"Not if I kill you first."

When Walker laughs, I have to fight to resist the urge to grab Aleks and run away with him.

"You think your threats will stop me? Give it your best shot. You pull it off, and my line lives on through my daughter. Ruby might deny me, but we're the same. In looks, in power, and in the need to control. We'll win this war, and my daughter will be the queen she was born to be. And all because of me."

Okay. If he wasn't already insane before his defeat, he sure as hell is now.

"There won't be any war," Aleks says firmly.

"Fine. Then give me the girl."

"No."

"No war. No mate."

Walker's voice has developed a teasing edge.

I'm immediately on guard. Something's not right. He's up to something.

"Aleks—"

"I came all this way in the snow. I should get something out of this." His eyes brighten suddenly, turning to molten lava in the moonlight. "I know." His hand slips behind him. When he pulls it back again, he's holding a gun that looks eerily familiar.

"I'm not as good as Christian. Maybe you'll get lucky, you fucking corpse."

Just like that, a bullet explodes out of the gun.

Aleks dodges it easily.

Another shot. Another miss.

My vampire gives him a look that clearly means, "Is that the best you can do?"

And that's when Walker turns the gun on me.

I instinctively know what's going to happen even as he pulls the trigger mercilessly. He was willing to throw two shots away to lull Aleks into a false sense of security because the Wicked Wolf doesn't hesitate to aim for my head.

I throw up my hands uselessly as Aleks jumps right in front of me.

One bullet, then a second punches his upper chest.

Bowing forward as soon as they hit, careful not to fall back against me even after he's been shot, Aleks drops to his knees, clutching his upper chest.

Not just bullets, I realize. Walker shot him with *silver* bullets.

And already they're hard at work, weakening him.

The satisfied look on the Alpha's face proves my suspicions true. He did that on purpose, using Aleks's protective instincts for me against him. He didn't want me dead—he just wanted me to be the reason that Aleks is incapacitated for the moment.

He keeps his gun aimed high with one hand. The other? He flexes it, releasing his deadly claws.

"It took an entire clip to capture him in the district," he says, so conversationally I can barely believe it. "Two already and he's down. I can keep going if you make me, Elizabeth. With enough silver in him, he won't be able to stop me from taking his head, either. I'll kill him."

He will. I know he will.

"Don't!"

It makes it so much worse that Walker derives pleasure from just how panicky my shout was.

He grins, and it's the most genuine smile I've ever seen apart from when he was lording over the deadly challenges in the pit. "See? I knew you wouldn't want that, not after he took those bullets for you. Leave with me and I spare him. Give me what I want or else I..."

Walker doesn't finish his threat. He doesn't have to. We both know exactly what he wants from me. What he's *always* wanted from me.

It's not just being his mate. The Alpha will throw me inside another gilded cage with him, but he won't be satisfied unless I turn the key myself.

What can I do? Peyton is still lying in the snow, and Aleks is on one knee, struggling to rise. Even after he took two bullets so that I didn't, he's doing everything he can to protect me.

He calls out my name—*my* name—but I force myself not to hear it.

What can I do?

To save the vampire I was born to love, I'll do *anything*.

I want him, but I can't have him. He'll find another. Julia. Gem. Me... he'll find another.

He always does.

I just wish, this time, it could've been *us*.

I'm sorry, Aleks. My apologies aren't as rare, but I can't bring myself to say it out loud as I approach him from behind. *I'm so, so sorry.*

Before he can figure out what I'm about to do, I lay my hand against his cheek.

Tapping into my wolf and the ability given to us by the Luna herself, I try to snap the thread tying us together.

It... it doesn't work.

Aleks's is normally cold to the touch. Not now. My hand is on fire.

No. Not just my hand. It's... every part of me.

I *burn*.

The last time this happened, the blowback was so powerful, a scream ripped out of my throat before my eyes rolled back in my head and I was out for a while. Grabbing Gem, trying to sever an unbreakable bond... I paid for breaking my promise to her.

We're not mated, me and Aleks. Not completely.

And while I have my doubts that it could ever work when I'm just another female's replacement, they're not enough to snap our fledgling bond.

My body burns, and I scream. Even as I realize that the tie between us is still there, the pain receding as quickly as it came, once again I pay for going against the Luna's will.

I crumple to the dirt. Still aware, still on fire, but at least I'm vaguely conscious enough to sense what's going on around me.

Aleks's answering bellow hits me like it's part of a dream.

I'll never know exactly what happened. My eyes were open, but unseeing. My wolf yowled in agony as the blowback hit her, burning the both of us, her screams drowning out Aleks's bellow, Peyton's screech, and Walker's excited yell.

My vampire has two bullets in him because of me. He's down one fang because of me. He just launched himself at a fierce enemy because of me.

And he manages to defeat him—because of me?

I don't know. What I *do* know, though?

Gem couldn't kill him. Showing her birth father mercy, she defeated him during their challenge before letting him go.

Aleks doesn't hesitate.

The Wicked Wolf of the West never stood a chance.

I'm still battling the aftershocks of my "gift" when it's all over and he's scooping me up in his arms, holding me against his wounded chest.

"Elizabeth? Elizabeth!" He reeks of blood—his own, and the bitter blood of the Alpha—but the cool touch on my cheek banishes the last of the burn. "Answer me, księżyca."

I blink a few times, desperately clearing my vision. When I do, all I see is his blood-stained shirt as he palms my head, keeping me from looking anywhere else. "Aleks?"

He sags to the ground with the both of us when he hears my weak voice. "I thought he'd killed you. I thought I failed you again."

"What? No… no. You didn't. It was me—"

"You tried to break our bond."

I don't deny it. I can't. "I… I had to."

"I lost my beloved once before. I won't lose you again."

"I'm not Julia," I whisper into his chest.

"No," he agrees. "But that doesn't change a thing I said."

I move my head just enough to see the stark look in his scarlet eyes. "Aleks—"

"I couldn't let him take you from me," he says, and I

can't tell if he's talking to himself or to me until he his voice roughens. "You're mine, Elizabeth."

I'm not, though. I might not have been able to sever the tentative bond between us because, deep down, neither of are ready to walk away from what we could have, but we don't have forever yet.

But my vampire is suddenly more fierce than I've ever seen him when he wasn't fighting. Red eyes on fire, blood staining the corner of his math, his hands spattered with gore...

The words catch in my throat. He accused me of denying him once before. And now... I just can't.

Aleks runs the back of his knuckles down my cheek. His skin stinks like Walker's blood, but I don't mind it. The Wicked Wolf is dead, and the predator inside of me revels in knowing who is responsible for the kill. My mate protected us, and my wolf whines to get closer to him.

I lean into his touch as I realize something I haven't denied in a while now.

I might not be his, but Aleks is *mine*.

Our bond isn't final—not yet—but it's undeniable. Suddenly, I want to tell him that we might have a shot at this. Peyton might be trouble, and I have my own issues to work out when it comes to being jealous of his past, but Jack Walker is no longer the bogeyman I search shadows for.

And all thanks to my vampire.

"Aleks… about the bond…"

"We'll talk about that later. Let's get your home first, then I must go see Roman and—"

At the mention of the lead vampire, I realize something else.

"Wait a second," I murmur, cutting him off. I thought the buzzing belonged to my skull, but as my regenerative properties continue to kick in, banishing the blowback from my curse, it's only getting more noticeable.

It's not buzzing. It's vibrating.

"Is that your phone?" I ask him.

He doesn't seem surprised at my question. In fact, he looks annoyed that someone might be trying to interrupt him. "Doesn't matter. They should be messaging me."

Only… it turns out that they have been.

Still holding me to him, Aleks pulls the phone out of his back pocket, jaw clenching as it stops vibrating. He doesn't hide the screen from me and, together, we see that he has six missed calls—and eleven messages—all from Cadre vampires.

I gulp. "Put me down."

"Are you sure?"

"I'm okay." Since he took the two bullets meant for my brain, I'm probably doing much better than he is. "You need to find out what's going on and deal with that."

He hesitates, but slowly shifts me so that I can stand on my own two feet.

"It wasn't pretty," he warns. "Behind me... I don't want you to see what I did."

He's still crouching in the dirt. At this level, I can easily brush one of his curls out of his face. It's sticky—more blood, I see—but that doesn't bother me.

My poor vampire obviously thinks I'm more fragile than I am. I might not be as strong as an alpha, but I'm still a shifter. Not only that, but for two years, I had to watch every challenge that Walker either hosted or took part in. The things I saw then ... I prayed to the Luna that he lost every single one, and when he finally did, Gem spared him.

Maybe I'm as bloodthirsty as Aleks, but I *need* to see that Walker is gone for good.

"I need to," I admit. "I need to see what you did to protect me."

My heart skips a beat as he vows solemnly, "I will always protect you, księżyca."

I press a quick kiss to his temple, then turn to take in the scene as Aleks—with a shaky, unnecessary breath—dials his phone.

He's watching me, searching for my reaction. It takes everything I have to take in the scene stoically, but... he was right. It's not pretty.

And I'm *glad*.

There's blood everywhere. It paints the snow a

deep, rich red, turning the dirt a darker shade where their brutal battle reveals the dirt. One lump of mangled flesh has to be Walker's remains. The blond head—forced from his shoulders, killing him—looks like it's been punted fifteen feet away like it was a football.

Peyton is gone, too. Not dead, like I'd secretly hopes, but vanished. Over the blood, I can't even pick up a hint of her scent trail as she bolted.

In the end, she was just as loyal to Walker as he was to her...

Behind me, the phone connects.

"Aleks." Dominic's voice thunders down the line. "They have Roman."

I spin so quickly, I nearly slip in the snow—or maybe that's blood. It doesn't matter.

"Roman?" I echo.

If they weren't before, Aleks's eyes are a blazing red with pure bloodlust. "What do you mean? They... who's they—no. It doesn't matter. If they have him, why haven't you gotten him back?"

Any time I met Dominic, he was suave. Put together. The male on the other end of the line is in a full-blown panic.

"We couldn't! None of us could, Aleksander."

"Why the hell not?"

"Because he forbade us from following after him and the wolf! All vampires in Muncie. But Cameron said you were checking the borders for a breach. For god's sake, tell me you're out of bounds."

Walker's remains are. That means that, at some point, Aleks was, too.

Would it work?

Only one way to find out.

I press my hand to his arm. He meets my gaze, nodding just the once.

"I was, but I'm coming back now. And I *will* find Roman."

Dominic said wolf, didn't he?

My loyal Beta is taking care of one...

Walker might be finished, but he isn't done.

I tilt my head back, showing him my black eyes. "We both will."

CHAPTER 18

In the middle of Muncie, there is a three-block square that is abandoned. I don't know why. It has some kind of bad history, and it's basically off-limits.

So of course that's where Walker's Beta dragged Roman off to.

Aleks guessed. Dominic only knew that a grim-faced shifter wearing a fang asked for a meeting with the head of the Cadre. Roman allowed him to come up to his office, and barely twenty minutes later, the wolf marched him out of the building at gunpoint.

Every member of the Cadre that was near obviously wanted to stop the determined wolf, but Roman refused to let them. He gave the orders that his vampires stand down, then left with the gun-toting shifter. Dominic and some others started calling and texting Aleks as soon as our boss was forced into a blacked-out dark red sedan and driven off.

While we were facing off with Walker, his Beta was doing exactly as the Alpha had boasted: he was being loyal to the end, and getting him his war.

Because even I know that if a wolf shifter harms the head vampire, there will be consequences.

From the second I heard that the Beta carried a gun, I knew who it had to be. It's not usual for a shifter to use human weapons, but Christian Morrissey—Walker's final Beta while he was the Alpha of the Western Pack—was... different. He was a marksman, too, with a skill that impressed even Walker.

The last time he faced off with Aleks, my vampire ended up with a bullet in each limb to incapacitate him. Aleks had been in a killing rage, fresh off of slaughtering his shifter opponent, and Christian hadn't batted an eye when Walker told his Beta to shoot him.

It hadn't killed him then, just like the bullets wouldn't kill Roman now. But with enough silver pumped inside of a vampire, the fanged supes turn docile. Weak.

Easy prey.

The sedan makes tracking Roman down nearly impossible. With the windows rolled up and the doors closed, neither one of them would leave a scent trail for us to follow. I have no tie to Christian, and Aleks has never taken either male's blood, so we can't track them by a bond.

We don't have to.

Aleks knows every inch of Muncie. Since it became a designated Fang City, he's considered it his territory. And though he doesn't spare time to explain why he's so sure that Christian would've driven Roman to the abandoned sector, when we spy the empty red car on the edge of it proving his hunch correct, Aleks doubles his speed. We've been running from the outskirts of Muncie, leaving any unaware humans who witness our flight in shock and awe. This is supernatural speed, and in any other situation, we would have to downplay our strengths when out on the streets.

Not now, though. Not while Roman needs us.

Aleks agrees. His scarlet eyes shining beneath the moonlight like freshly spilled blood, he pushes himself to his limit; even with the silver blazing inside of him, he's faster than me. Tapping into my wolf, I work hard to close the gap between us.

Aleks rasps out another couple of words in Polish —*nie ty*— before gesturing for me to fall back. Shaking my head, I stay right beside him.

I almost lost him once. After our confrontation with Walker, I don't want to let Aleks out of my sight.

He's too focused on our pursuit to argue. I don't blame him. I can't let Christian hurt Roman. The head vampire has been so good to me, allowing me to live here, giving me a job, even subtly nudging me and Aleks together… would Walker and his Beta even have turned their sights on Muncie if it wasn't for me? Maybe, because of Gem's ties here, but he hadn't attacked Accalia, had he? He'd gone after *us*.

As I run, I'm constantly stretching out my senses. Breathing in deep, I finally catch a hint of their scents on the breeze. Roman and, like I thought, *Christian*.

Now, if I can, Aleks probably does, too, but I still grab his arm.

He spares me a quick glance. As beautiful as he is fierce, I swallow a lump in my throat before stammering out, "Up ahead. I can scent them."

A quick nod. "We go to the left then."

I get it. Instead of walking into what might be a trap, we'll circle around and approach them from behind. With my ability to conceal scents from those near me, it'll be a way to catch them off guard. I normally have to focus to use that part of my "gift", but as soon as Walker lured us to the edge of Muncie, I'd triggered it almost subconsciously for both me and Aleks.

For once, my curse can help me instead of hurt me. We know where Christian has Roman, but he won't know we've tracked him down until he sees us.

Hopefully, it'll buy us some time.

The two of us slow down as we take the last corner,

only for Aleks to lose control and fly down the street when he finally spies Roman.

The noble vampire has his hands bound behind him. He's still standing, perched on the corner at the other end of the block. Christian is at his back, the mouth of his gun against Roman's head.

Aleks hisses. My wolf reacts by letting out a yip when we realize just how real the danger to Roman is. Being shot in the head probably won't kill him, but it might. And if it didn't? It would definitely put him down long enough for Christian to grab the hilt of the sword he has strapped to his back.

We stop when there's less than a block separating us—and not because we want to.

It's Roman. His aura pulses, a warning to both of us to stay away. It's enough to have my wolf howling, desperate to turn tail and get the hell out of here, but Aleks?

He staggers backward. It's like some invisible hand shoved him away so that he can't get any closer to where Christian has the gun pressed to Roman's temple.

And the only one strong enough to do that? Is the head vampire himself.

Ever since I met Roman Zakharov, I couldn't understand why everyone in Muncie treated him like a bogeyman. Even Gem did. I knew he was the leader of Muncie's Cadre, so it was a given he had to be powerful. I just had no idea *how* powerful until he unleashed his aura on us.

Suddenly, Dominic's panic makes a lot more sense. Roman had forbidden any of his people from following him. If that wall of power was what they were up against, no way could they disobey him. They physically couldn't go after him.

But Christian is a beta wolf. Strong, but nowhere near strong enough to defeat Roman even if he used his gun. He had Roman trussed up, his hands probably tied with a length of silver chain, but Roman had still been able to use his aura against me and Aleks.

The only reason he's over there is because he's *choosing* to be.

"Aleksander," he calls out, oddly conversational. "I didn't want any of you to witness this."

Understanding hits, slamming into me so hard it's like an anvil's been dropped on my head. Barely an hour ago, I was running with Aleks, heading to the border to face off against the unknown threat breaching our borders. I'd thought then that Roman had orchestrated the meeting; when it was revealed that Walker was waiting for us, I was sure of it. Now? I realize that Roman's moves were even more subtle than I expected.

Not only did he give Aleks his chance at revenge, he also got him out of his hair so that he could do something as ridiculously noble as this.

I'm glad your wait is over... mine is, too...

Did he know he would be doing this tonight?

I... I think he did.

Aleks is frantic. Palms outstretched, he tests the barrier that Roman's thrown up, growling under his breath when he can't get past it. He grunts and he shoves and he pushes before he hunches his shoulder, imploring Roman with his gaze.

His soft voice lowers an octave as he calls out, "Drop your shields. Let me get to you."

"I can not." When Aleks immediately starts to argue, Roman shakes his head. "No. I *will* not. I gave my word."

"Your word? Your word about what? Roman, stop this!"

"Didn't you hear him? He won't," Christian cuts in. "And even if he would, *I* can't let him."

Before any of us can react, he kicks Roman's legs out from under him, forcing him to his knees.

Roman's aura falters. Either that, or the rage pouring off of my vampire is so strong that—even with two bullets inside of him—he can push past it.

"Nyet," yells Roman sharply. *No.* What comes next is a rattle of Russian that means nothing to me, even as I buckle under the weight of its obvious command. "Odna zhizn' na besschetnoye kolichestvo. Ya delayu eto dlya nashego naroda. Ty dolzhen pozvolit' mne, staryy drug!"

I have no idea what he said, but my vampire?

He goes immovably still. After swallowing roughly, he says, "Wolf. Why do you do this? Roman has only ever sought peace between our kinds."

"That's exactly my point," Christian answers. "He might want peace." With Roman on his knees, Christian moved the gun to the back of his skull. Using his free hand, he strokes the fang hanging off of his neck. "There are plenty who don't. Other vampires want his head. I'm more than happy to give it to them."

"But *why*?"

"Because the rebels have given their word that they will stop rising up against the Cadre with my death," answers Roman. He juts his chin out even as Christian hovers over him. "One for many. I give my life gladly."

"You don't have to do that!"

"Of course he does," Christian tells Aleks. "And it would've been done already if you hadn't interrupted." His dark eyes turn toward me. "Where is he, Elizabeth?"

I don't have to ask who he means. "He's dead."

The Beta doesn't look the least bit surprised to hear that. In fact, he looks… *satisfied*?

But then his brow furrows. "Who killed him? You or—"

"He threatened my beloved."

Aleks hunches slightly as he bites the words out, his hands clenched into fists at his side. His aura is electric against my skin, but it doesn't hurt. It feels familiar to me. Safe. As if he'll do that and more to anyone who dares threaten me.

Instead of realizing that Aleks is already plotting to take him out next, Christian's eyes light up, echoing the insanity I saw in the Wicked Wolf's gaze before he goaded my vampire to attack him. "Then the Alpha got just what he wanted. Dead at the hand of a parasite."

I was right. They planned this. Walker. Christian.

Roman.

This end was inevitable. That doesn't keep me from calling out to the Luna, beseeching my goddess, hoping for Roman's sake—for *Aleks's* sake—that broken, battered, hopeless Elizabeth can do something to stop this.

But I can't. If the Luna hears me, she doesn't answer, and both males on the other side of Roman's barrier are determined.

Reaching behind him, Christian grabs the hilt peeking over his shoulder. In one practiced motion, he unsheathes it.

I stop breathing.

Roman might survive a gunshot to the head. But a blade to the neck?

Never.

Christian's banking on it, too. "Now all I need is the top parasite taken down by one of my kind and he'll have his war." Kneeing Roman in the back, he sneers, "Say your goodbyes."

Roman is regal to the end. "We'll meet again one day, Aleksander. And Elizabeth. It was a pleasure to know you both." I barely stifle my sob as he holds his head high before addressing Aleks again. "Until then, you know what's expected of you."

Aleks doesn't deny it. Though every muscle in his body strains to go to him, he stays where he is, even as he rumbles, "It doesn't have to end like this."

"Enjoy your beloved, sobrat. And don't worry for me. I look forward to seeing my Kira again."

Aleks opens his mouth, but nothing comes out. He just gives Christian a murderous glare. "Don't do this. Please."

"Too late."

Christian swings his sword. Aleks immediately grabs me, tucking me into his side. Burying my head against his chest, I close my eyes so I don't see what happens next.

I hear it, though. The whistle of the blade, the thud as Roman's head is separated from his shoulders, the pained grunt as Aleks stands there, watching as his friend—his brother—sacrifices his life for his people.

Aleks's body bucks, almost as if he physically felt the same blow. Then, suddenly, his arms are clutching my shoulders, whirling me away before shoving me behind me. With my eyes screwed shut, I have no idea what's going on. I let out a cry of surprise as I stumble forward, righting myself at the same time as my eyes spring open again.

I'm facing away from Aleks. Spinning around, I discover exactly why Aleks pushed me away.

Christian dropped his bloody sword, trading it for his gun again. Now that Roman is... is *gone*, he's turned his attention on us. And since Aleks's instincts are to protect me, he's using his body as a shield.

I'm a wolf. My instincts are shouting at me to do the same thing for him.

I reach for him, screaming when the first crack of gunfire explodes through the night.

Boom.

Boom.

Boom.

Boom.

Boom.

With an impassive expression on his sallow face, Christian doesn't hesitate as he plugs Aleks full of silver. Two bullets dead to the chest, one in each thigh, and a single shot in his right shoulder.

That last one has Aleks bellowing in pain as the force of the hit has him rearing back before dropping to his knees.

He pounds the asphalt with his left fist, hissing out a stream of Polish too fast for me to recognize any of it except for one single word: zabić.

Kill.

Christian lowers the gun. "Threaten me all you want. You can't do anything about it now, and I fulfilled my word to your headless leader by letting you live tonight. The next time we meet? You won't be so lucky."

"Me?" Aleks's normally gentle voice is a hoarse rasp. "I'll pluck your spine from you and make you see it before I drain you."

"Big talk for someone full of silver. You can't even get out of the dirt."

He isn't wrong. Though Aleks's aura crackles and pulses with obvious rage, he's still down. He might've been able to push past Walker's two bullets, but five more? Until he expels them from his body, he's no match for another supe and we both know it.

That doesn't mean I'm going to leave my proud vampire on the ground. Throwing Christian a look of tear-filled loathing, I dash toward Aleks, intent on helping him to his feet.

He throws his left arm—the only part of him that's unwounded—behind him. "Stay back, księżyca. Don't come any closer."

What?

Why?

Oh.

For the second time tonight, I'm staring down the

barrel of a gun. And, just like before, I know that the bullet is aimed right at me.

Christian has strode forward, arm outstretched, hand completely steady. His dark eyes are focused on me, Aleks forgotten as he says in an emotionless tone, "I saved this one for you."

My breath catches in my throat.

He smiles. "I bargained for that parasite's life. But you, Elizabeth... Alpha never would've wanted you to bond with a bloodsucker. This is for him."

"But he's dead!"

"Now it's your turn."

My wolf whimpers, my instincts telling me to move. I *can't*.

Aleks has seven silver bullets in him. He's on his knees, bowed beneath grief and pain. Even so, as his blood-red eyes lock on Christian's steady hand, he forces himself to get up.

The beta's head swivels to look at him. His smile thins into a line of grim determination. He's fighting the urge to fire on Aleks again.

He claims there's only one bullet left. Would Aleks survive an eighth hit? Maybe, but he shouldn't have to. He's already taken seven for me.

I'll take this one for him.

Save him, commands the Luna. She only echoes my own instincts. *Save your mate.*

One step away from Aleks, another step toward the beta, purposely drawing his attention back to me. That's all I manage before Christian's finger jerks on the trigger, the bullet exploding out of his gun.

I'm a supe. Silver is excruciatingly painful to all of us, but shifters—especially wolves—have a weakness to the metal. A single bullet isn't enough to kill me; it'll only make me wish it had. If Aleks can still move with *seven* bullets, I can handle one.

And I believe that until Christian's bullet unerringly pierces my heart.

With Aleks's roar of rage blowing out my eardrums, I gasp a single breath as everything around me goes hazy and dim. The pain is indescribable—but it doesn't last. My whole body seizes, and suddenly I'm falling, falling, falling.

My heart stops beating even before I hit the ground.

EPILOGUE

I thought I was dead. In fact, I was sure of it.

I'm not.

It was a close call, though. Two days later, when I wake up in a hospital bed, a red-eyed Aleks sitting at my bedside, I realize just how close it was. If my vampire hadn't gotten me to the supe hospital in Muncie in time, I would've died on the street.

Just like Roman had.

Christian knew what he was doing. Either he killed me, getting revenge for Walker's death, or he wounded me bad enough that Aleks would be forced to choose between saving me or avenging Roman's murder.

He chose me. When Roman died, his aura died with him, and Aleks could have gone after Christian. Instead, he scooped me up, carrying me out of the abandoned sector where he flagged down the first vampire he met who was in a vehicle. Shuffling me in the backseat with him, he commanded the female to drive us to the hospital—all while Christian took the opportunity to get away.

He hadn't left my side since. When I woke up again, the first thing I asked about was Roman. With a pained expression, he told me that Dominic is taking care of everything right now, and that all I needed to worry about was recovering from surgery.

That's right. To repair the damage the silver bullet did to my heart, I had to have surgery. A team of humans in the know worked on me, putting my heart back together so that my regenerative properties could heal the near-fatal wound.

I should've been dead. And when I murmur that out loud, Aleks shudders.

He knows I'm right.

I've never seen him like this. So... defeated. Even when he was thrown in the pit, he was defiant and unstoppable. Slumped in the hospital chair, telling me what happened after I went unconscious because I begged him to... this isn't the Aleksander Filan I know.

And my newly repaired heart aches for him.

"It's going to be okay," I lie. Because how can it? Walker is dead, but so is Roman. Christian and Peyton made it out of Muncie, and from the whispers I overheard when I was semi-conscious before waking fully earlier, Aleks and Dominic have been discussing the vampires that resist the Cadre's leadership. The rebels Roman mentioned before he—

Before he—

I struggle to bring a weak grin to my face as I echo softly, "It'll be okay."

He nods, a single curl falling forward, brushing against his upper cheek. "Now that you're awake again, it will be."

There's something in the way he says that. Almost like he's been sitting vigil, expecting me to die in front of him.

Just like Julia did.

I should've—and I'm still not so sure why I didn't.

"How... how did I make it? When I fell, I thought that was it for me."

"Tak. And it would've been only... I fed you my blood." He pauses, as if unsure how I'm going to react when he adds, "A lot of my blood. It kept you alive until I could get you to the surgeons. I would've done anything to bring you back."

Bring you back...

Panic flares up in me. I tamp it down, even though I can't stop myself from asking, "Am I a vampire now?"

"What? No. You'd have to die to be turned. And it was close, mój księżyca, but you never died." A fierce expression twists his features. "I wouldn't let you."

Okay, then.

In that case, I don't see what the problem is. Aleks

is looking at me like I'm already dead, or if he's lost me for good.

But I'm right here.

Most supes can survive being shot. Taking a silver bullet to the heart, though? I should be dead. If it wasn't for Aleks, I would be. He kept me alive, he got me to help, and he stayed right next to me the whole time.

"You saved my life."

Aleks leans forward in his seat, gingerly taking my hand in his. "It's only fair. You *are* my life."

I squeeze. For months, I refused to believe what my instincts were telling me. I stayed away from Aleks, only moving to Muncie when I felt like I had no other choice. Even then I ignored him, then rejected him, before finally allowing myself to think that maybe Fate had gotten it right after all.

I might be Aleks's second chance, but he's my only hope.

Meeting his red eyes, I ask, "What happens now?"

"Nothing. At least, not until you're all better. We'll figure out what comes next later." The unnatural shade of his irises grows impossibly deeper. "Together."

Nodding in agreement when it becomes obvious that he's expecting an answer, I try to hide my sudden discomfort. My stomach tightens and my throat grows dry as I realize something.

When I asked my question, I wasn't only talking to

him. I was asking the Luna what Fate has in store for us.

But, for the first time that I can remember, she doesn't answer me.

The goddess who's been my constant companion has gone silent, and I have no idea what that means—only that it can't be good...

AUTHOR'S NOTE

Thanks for reading *Hint of Her Blood*!

This is the first of two books devoted to Elizabeth and Aleks. So while this part of their story ends with a HFN — happy for now — when it comes to their relationship, they will eventually have their HEA — happily ever after — at the close of the next release in this series, *Taste of His Skin*, coming out in August.

The Wicked Wolf might finally be gone, but he's left a devoted Beta in his wake, as well as a scorned female who has her own reasons to make Elizabeth pay.

Not to mention the power vacuum left behind with poor Roman's murder...

The next book will close out this arc. After that, I have at least one more planned in this world — featuring Duke and Trish — as well as the new series launching in the same universe, **Stolen Mates.** *The Feral's Captive* comes out in June, but that's not all :)

Keep scrolling/clicking/reading to find out what else I have in store for you!

xoxo,
Sarah

PRE-ORDER NOW
TASTE OF HIS SKIN

The first time his beloved died, he waged a war for her. If my vampire is not careful, he'll do it all over again...

The Wicked Wolf is dead, but the price we paid for his death was way more than either me and Aleks could afford.

As the new head vampire in Muncie, Aleks is suddenly busier than ever before. I might wear his fang and sleep in his bed, but I rarely see him. He hasn't asked me to accept him fully as his mate again, and I can't shake the feeling that he's still comparing me to his lost female.

Meanwhile, I have my own war to wage. When Peyton follows through with Walker's threat to out me to the Alpha collective, the truth of my abilities finally get out the whole shifter world.

Now I've got an even bigger target on my back. When a group of shifters decide that I'm too much of a risk to be allowed to stay alive, they come after me. And they're not the only ones.

To protect me, Aleks decides that it's time I take him as my bonded mate. And I want to—but I can't. The Luna has gone silent, and without her blessing, the bond won't take.

So I reject him one last time, and then I do the only thing I've ever been good at: I run away.

There's just one small problem. He might not have claimed me, but all it took was one bite—one taste of his skin—and I've inadvertently triggered a vampire's blood bonding.

And Aleks? He's willing to burn down the whole world to find me.

** *Taste of His Skin* is the conclusion of Aleks and Elizabeth's arc in the **Claws and Fangs** series. With Elizabeth struggling to accept that Aleks wants to take her as his beloved, she uses the looming Claws and Fangs war to reject him in a bid to save her heart. Too late does she realize she's already given it away—and Aleks isn't about to let her take it back. For two hundred years he waited for his second chance, and he found it in a haunted female who needs him to save her.

So he *will*.

Releasing August 16, 2022

PRE-ORDER NOW

MATED TO THE MONSTER

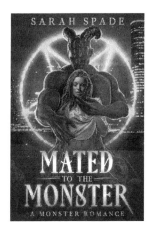

I really should've known better than to play around with that spell book...

How was I supposed to know that the incantations scrawled inside of it worked? That the first one I read would open a portal into a demon plane — or that the next one was an unbreakable vow to the seven foot tall shadow monster I unwittingly summoned into my bedroom?

He says his name is Malphas, that he's something called a Sombra demon, and I'm his mate.

Monster, demon... whatever he is, his muscles are bigger than my head, and that club between his legs... I don't know if *mate* means the same thing to him as it does me, but he's gotta be kidding.

Spoiler alert: he's *not*.

Mal has been waiting for more than a thousand years for the one woman meant for him. He's convinced that's me, and he's willing to do anything to prove it. And maybe there's something really wrong with me because, before long, I find myself eager to let him try...

* *Mated to the Monster* is the first in a series about the Sombra demons, a race of shadow-based monsters who will do anything to claim their females. Mal and Shannon might come from different worlds, but when it comes to fate, lust, and forever... they might just be a perfect match.

Out May 24, 2022

KEEP IN TOUCH

Stay tuned for what's coming up next! Sign up for my mailing list for news, promotions, upcoming releases, and more!

Sarah Spade's Stories

And make sure to check out my Facebook page for all release news:

http://facebook.com/sarahspadebooks

Sarah Spade is a pen name that I used specifically to write these holiday-based novellas (as well as a few books that will be coming out in the future). If you're interested in reading other books that I've written (romantic suspense, Greek mythology-based romance, shifters/vampires/witches romance, and fae romance), check out my primary author account here:

http://amazon.com/author/jessicalynch

ALSO BY SARAH SPADE

Holiday Hunk

Halloween Boo

This Christmas

Auld Lang Mine

I'm With Cupid

Getting Lucky

When Sparks Fly

Holiday Hunk: the Complete Series

Claws and Fangs

Leave Janelle

Never His Mate

Always Her Mate

Forever Mates

Hint of Her Blood

Taste of His Skin

Stay With Me

Sombra Demons

Mated to the Monster

Stolen to the Shadows

Stolen Mates

The Feral's Captive

The Beta's Bride

Claws Clause

(written as Jessica Lynch)

Mates *free*

Hungry Like a Wolf

Of Mistletoe and Mating

No Way

Season of the Witch

Rogue

Sunglasses at Night

Ain't No Angel *free*

True Angel

Ghost of Jealousy

Night Angel

Broken Wings

Of Santa and Slaying

Lost Angel

Born to Run

Uptown Girl

Ordinance 7304: the Bond Laws (Claws Clause Collection #1)

Living on a Prayer (Claws Clause Collection #2)

Printed in Great Britain
by Amazon